MURDER in Mobile

An Alex Trotter Mystery

Cheryl Peyton

ISBN -13: 979-8715266736
ISBN -

This book was printed in the United States of America, 2021.

Other books by Cheryl Peyton

Six Minutes to Midnight

Walk on Through the Rain: A Polio Survivor's Story

Murder on Bedford Island (introducing Alex Trotter)

Murder on the Bermuda Queen: An Alex Trotter Mystery

Murder in Margaritaville: An Alex Trotter Mystery

Murder in Montmartre: An Alex Trotter Mystery

Murder on the Rhine: An Alex Trotter Mystery

Conversation with Cody: A Sassy Canine Speaks his Mind

Wigged Out! Surviving Chemo and Other Intrusions

Available on Amazon in soft cover and as an Ebook for Kindle.
In soft cover at www.barnesandnoble.com
Available also at www.authorsguildoftn.org

Chapter 1

ALEX slid down the kitchen cabinet to come to rest on the floor. Her head lolled forward in defeat as she squeezed her eyes shut. "Rosemary, I think that may be stalking, even if he is your husband. I'll ask Arlie if what you're doing is even legal."

Detective Arlie Tate looked up from the morning paper as he sat at the dining room table. Peering through the kitchen doorway, he focused his attention on his wife.

Alex had stretched her legs and leaned back. "Of course, you could ask Mitch, but that probably isn't a good idea." There was a pause. "What? I understand that. I know his actions are suspicious, but I don't think you should put a GPS on his car or some gizmo on his computer or whatever."

The conversation continued a few more minutes. "Let's leave it there for now. We'll talk more after I get to Mobile. I should be at the Granada about three . . . oh, that's right, you're an hour behind. Make that two. You want me to call you when I arrive? Okay, I'll just expect you sometime after two. That's fine. Can't wait to see you and the others."

Arlie strolled into the kitchen, reached out and pulled her to her feet. "What was *that* all about?" he drawled in his native Atlanta accent.

"I'll *tell* you what *that* all about," Alex parroted as she dropped his hands and headed for the dining room. "*That* was the death knell to our reunion, that's what *that* was."

"That's a little dramatic," Arlie commented from the doorway.

"Not any more than it really is." Alex pulled out a chair from the table and perched on the front edge. "You know we've been planning this get-together for months and now Rosemary has a marital crisis that's making her half-crazy."

"Sorry, but which one is Rosemary again?" Tilting his head toward the kitchen, he added, "You want some more coffee?"

Alex flipped a hand indifferently. "Sure. Couldn't hurt."

Moments later he entered the dining room carrying a carafe. After filling both cups, he sat and looked at his wife expectantly.

Alex shook her head to bring her mind back to his question. "Uh, Rosemary's the shy one who's very pretty. In a Renaissance sort of way."

Arlie blinked. "Whatever that means. I don't think she sounds very shy from what I heard on your end."

"She's shy around strangers, but she has a passionate personality when you get to know her. And right now, she wants to kill her husband for cheating on her; not that she even knows if it's true."

Arlie took a moment. "Hmmm. That would be Mitch."

"Yeah. He's a prominent lawyer in Mobile."

"What kind of lawyer?"

"The prosecuting kind. He's actually the District Attorney for Mobile County—a very influential guy. I think Rosemary should be careful."

"I think you're right. To answer the questions you haven't asked — yes, it's illegal to put a GPS on someone's car without a court order. And, yes, you can be convicted of stalking a spouse, although, usually, it's an ex-spouse. She should also know that any evidence from spying could be inadmissible in court."

Alex crossed her arms and made a low guttural sound. "This is just great. I haven't seen these people in ten years, and now all we'll be doing is commiserating with Rosemary, or, worse yet, be sent out as spies."

Arlie checked his smile. "Why don't you put off your reunion for a while? Rosemary will either make up with the guy or divorce him."

Alex stared at him, wide-eyed. "We can't reschedule. It's Mardi Gras week in Mobile. That's the whole point of our getting together there now."

"Oh, yeah. Sorry. I forgot."

Alex leaned forward, resting on her elbows. "You can't believe what a big deal this is. I told you that Mobile is where the whole Mardi Gras thing began years before New Orleans. In Mobile, they start on Thanksgiving with a debutante ball, long before the season's supposed to begin on Epiphany."

"Sounds more like an excuse for rich people to party," Arlie opined.

"That dance is just for the elite, but this week is when all the secret societies put on their balls, inviting hundreds of people."

Arlie topped off her cup. "Which ball are you going to, again?"

"Rosemary got us tickets to hers—the 'Mystic Goddesses'," Alex answered with an eye roll, then took a sip of coffee.

"So . . . you can go just as you are, without a costume."

Alex sputtered on her mouthful. "Funny. Actually, only the members wear costumes with masks so no one can know who they are, supposedly. As for the guests, the men are expected to wear tails and the women, long gowns."

Arlie shook his head. "Between the parties and the parades and hanging out with all of you, Rosemary'll forget about her problems with Mitch while you're there."

Alex smiled wanly. "Hah. From your mouth to the Goddesses' ears."

Chapter 2

"BE SURE YOU CALL ME when you get there," Arlie advised for the third time that morning as he lowered the tailgate of her Subaru in the building's garage.

Alex stood by her door on the driver's side. "I will, I will. I'll be fine. It's only a five-hour drive and there shouldn't be much traffic on the interstates on Sunday."

He came around the side of the car, put his hands firmly on her shoulders and looked her in the eye. "I know you're more than capable. I just like hearing from you."

Alex responded with a quick hug. "I know. I'll probably be calling you several times over the next five days so you can follow the action. I don't know what to expect and I'm usually the one who's in charge, making all the plans for a group visiting some place. I can't remember the last time I wasn't."

"Our honeymoon," Arlie answered dryly without missing a beat.

Alex looked properly sheepish. "Oh, right. Well, this won't be anything like that."

"I hope not. Besides the obvious, you almost got yourself killed that week trying to catch a murderer. Not everyone's idea of a romantic getaway." Arlie opened the driver's door.

Alex tossed her purse over to the passenger seat and turned back to him, shaking her head. "You always bring up the *few* murders that have happened on my tours—but only when you're along. No offense."

"None taken. It's not *me*. If you'll recall, I met you when I was sent out to investigate the murder of one of your people when you were staying on Bedford Island. In fact, you were my first suspect." He grinned broadly.

Alex waved her hand dismissively. "Okay, okay. Let's not go back over that. Give me a kiss and I'll be on my way. I'll call you this afternoon."

Arlie held her face and brought his lips down to hers, lingering for several seconds, then patted her cheek. "Take care, babe. Have a good trip, y'hear?"

Alex slid under the steering wheel, smiling at the southern expression. She was still amused by local idioms having lived in Chicago all her life until she married Arlie last year and moved to Atlanta.

Fluttering her fingers at him out the car window, she maneuvered the vehicle out of the parking garage and onto Oak Valley Road to make her way over to the interstate

A few minutes later she was driving onto the on-ramp to I-85, *en route* to Montgomery where she'd pick up I-65 to take her into Mobile.

As expected, traffic was light. Driving was made even easier with a light cloud cover that reduced the glare on the roadway and also kept the air chilly.

Turning the radio on to a pop music station, she turned her thoughts to her college friends she would be seeing for the first time since they had graduated ten years earlier. Considering they had been roommates in adjacent dorm rooms for two years, then moved to Terrace House off-campus for the last two years, she felt they should be able to reconnect and relate to one another as they had in school. Since Woodley was a women's college, offering few dating opportunities, the five of them had spent most of their social time together.

Hopefully, Arlie was right that Rosemary would be so distracted by the Mardi Gras activities and reuniting with her friends that she could put aside her troubles for a few days.

Rosemary had always been a sweet, soft-spoken young woman, but Alex remembered, too, her flashes of temper. Usually, there was just cause—a new school policy that didn't make sense, or some tedious assignment from her psychology professor. Her favorite expression when she was riled was, "Holy crap!" Alex hadn't thought about that in years, but in her mind, she could still hear Rosemary's voice saying that.

Rosemary had been roommates with Millie, a pint-sized pixie from Ohio. Although she still looked like a naive young girl, she was one smart cookie and was sophisticated beyond her years and life experience.

Physically, she was petite, with a muscular, athletic build that matched her feisty personality. Never one to back down from a challenge, she had proven herself to be competent in handling whatever difficulties had come her way. Never more so than on one September night in their junior year, when she had demonstrated to her friends at Terrace House that she could protect them as well.

As Alex drove into Birmingham and followed the signs to pick up I-65, she thought back to that incident. She and her roommate Josie had been awakened in the middle of the night by loud voices, thumping sounds and muffled footsteps coming from upstairs. Sitting bolt upright in their beds, they shared a shocked, puzzled look, and then headed for the door of their first-floor room.

Rounding the corner behind the staircase, they recognized Millie's voice shouting at someone. "Get outta here, you creep! What do you think you're doing, pervert?!"

From the bottom step, Alex and Josie peered up into the near-darkness, unable to see anything. After a few moments, they could make out a man scuttling down the stairs towards them with his hands held protectively over his head. Millie was right behind him brandishing a closed umbrella like a rapier.

"Ouch! Ouch! I'm leaving!" the man cried out, as her weapon found its mark.

Alex and Josie jumped back behind the newel post as the man crashed onto the floor at the bottom of the stairs, curled up into a fetal position with his trench coat pulled up over his head.

Millie wasn't done with him. Standing over the immobile figure she spat out, "And don't come back!" as she made one last riposte at the man's head causing him to cry out in pain.

"Please! Stop! You're going to kill me!" he wailed.

Just then, housemother Dean Merrill rushed onto the scene, tying the sash of her blue terry robe "Don't move!" she commanded the now blubbering intruder. "I've called the police. They'll be here in two minutes."

By this time, the other nine girls in the house had come out of their rooms, with several of them coming down to the landing above the scene where they remained, staring in disbelief.

Looking up at them, Alex couldn't be sure if they were shocked by seeing an intruder or by what they had witnessed of Millie's assault.

As Dean Merrill promised, within two minutes the women heard sirens followed by blue and white lights flashing through the windows.

Alex recalled how her heart had raced with the excitement.

Dean Merrill took one last look at the quaking figure on the floor before she spun around and hurried to answer the insistent knocking on the front door.

A solemn man's voice said from the other side, "Campus police. Open the door."

Flipping the wall switch for the porch light, the dean flung the door open to reveal two solid-looking, uniformed cops, their features in shadow under their hat brims.

"Dean Merrill?" one asked.

"Yes, come in." she answered with relief in her voice. "We're all right. One of the girls was able to subdue the man."

That seemed like an understatement to Alex. To an observer just coming upon the scene, the prowler could have easily been mistaken for the victim, if one took into account who stood confidently *en garde* with an umbrella and who lay in a heap, sobbing on the floor.

When the police turned the man over, Millie cried out, "Hah! It's Lawson! I'm not surprised."

The heavier cop pulled the known exhibitionist up by his coat collar high enough to look into his face. "What are you doing here, John? As if I didn't know."

As the cop helped the man to his feet, his trench coat flipped open to one side, exposing what he had intended to show the women. "And keep this wrapped around yourself. No one's in the mood to see your, uh . . . charms right now."

The second officer tied the coat's belt around the intruder's waist to cover him adequately. "With your record, this is probably worth ninety days. Aren't you ever going to learn?"

"I just wanted to touch her, that's all," Lawson whimpered. "I didn't mean any harm."

"Of course not. You never do."

With the prowler covered up, the partner then handcuffed and controlled his prisoner by solidly grasping his upper right arm. "You want to expose yourself to all the young women on campus, and in the process, you scare them half to death. If you didn't already know, you're under arrest for burglary, sexual misconduct, and 'passing on the right' if I can make it stick."

He turned to his partner. "Lou, let's get this guy down to the station. Ladies, sorry he bothered you."

After the police left with John Lawson in custody, the girls stayed up for the next two hours going over every detail of the event, speculating on how the local flasher got inside the house, deciding he must have gotten in the side door before they had locked it for the night. Then he could have hidden downstairs in the kitchen, or elsewhere in the basement, until everyone had gone to bed.

John Lawson's reputation had preceded his visit to Terrace House. It was general knowledge among the students of Woodley that his typical modus operandi was to enter an off-campus house or a dorm on campus during daytime hours, hide in a closet or bath stall, then sneak into one of the dorm rooms and stroke the arms or legs of a sleeping student until she woke up. Usually, the girl would scream and he'd run, oftentimes avoiding capture.

This night he had made the wrong choice of a victim. Millie had fearlessly gone on the attack. As she had told her riveted audience that night, as soon as she awakened from his touch, she punched him in the face as hard as she could, knocking him to the floor. Before he could get up, she had found her umbrella and aimed the tip at his private parts. As he got to his feet, she rammed him into a wall, then grabbed him and started stabbing him with the end of the umbrella, pursuing him down the stairs.

The story of Millie's assault on Lawson spread across the campus the next day, making her a local hero. Alex felt that Millie's action probably gave confidence to all the young women in the school that they could defend themselves against this sick character if he should appear in their rooms.

* * *

Millie was the only one of the five–attending this reunion in Mobile who hadn't yet married. She had been working as a foreign correspondent, calling her stories into the television networks from hotspots around the world. When she was home, she lived in Lexington, Kentucky.

Josie lived in the city with the same name in Virginia. Alex hadn't seen her roommate since she had stood up in her wedding as her Maid of Honor the summer after graduation. Thinking about that brought back a memory of the times living with her at Terrace House.

Josie had been regarded as the most disciplined, level-headed, and sensible of all the residents in the house.

Known as a brilliant student, she studied in isolation every night, always turned in course work on time, and made the Dean's list every semester.

Josie showed self-control in all areas of her life, including being frugal with her money. She never bought anything extravagant or frivolous. Alex had been surprised to learn she came from a wealthy family, and that her home was a Tudor mansion cared for by live-in help.

Considering her temperance in all things, Josie's impulsive act in their junior year caught everyone off guard.

One day, in the fall of that year, Marshall Higgins, a young man who lived across the street in his parents' home, issued an open invitation to anyone at Terrace House to be his guest for a one-week vacation at a resort in Bimini, all expenses paid.

Two of the girls had gone out with Marshall once or twice and liked him, but didn't feel comfortable with the commitment of a full week. No one else in the house was acquainted with him, except to say 'hi' if they saw him in the neighborhood.

That same day, Josie shocked everyone when she announced that she had accepted his offer.

When asked why, she had shrugged and responded with her usual practical rationale: "Why not?" How else would she get a free trip to a luxurious resort on a tropical island, she asked. No one could refute the logic and everyone suddenly doubted the wisdom of their own decision to decline the offer.

During the week when Josie and Marshall were away, it was all anyone in the house could talk about. Speculations on how the week was going ran the gamut from the couple enduring awkward silences to their falling madly in love.

When Josie was due back from the airport, everyone gathered in the living room of Terrace House to welcome her home, hopefully to hear a full and juicy account of the week. As she lumbered in tanned and glowing with her luggage and souvenirs, they stared expectantly at her, waiting to hear what she had to say for herself. But her only response was to smile and say, 'hi.' Given Josie's typical reserve, no one dared asked for intimate details. As she headed off to her room, she said over her shoulder, "Oh, we had a good time. It was a lot of fun."

In the weeks that followed, it became obvious that Josie and Marshall had fallen in love. Josie continued to look radiant, carefully dressing in her best outfits and wearing her hair up in a new flattering style. Marshall also looked happy when he came by the house every weekend to take her out on dates.

In their senior year, they became engaged. A month after graduation, they were married in a lavish country-club wedding. Now, ten years later, the couple was still happily married and had a young son.

Thinking about the streamlined way Josie and Marshall had gotten together, Alex thought about Dottie's erratic love life when she had been at Terrace House.

As she drove, Alex conjured up an image of Dottie from back then, seeing her telling a funny anecdote, her voice light with laughter, her face creased in amusement. Dottie had the sunniest disposition of the five of them.

When the group first became friends in Smith Hall during their freshman year, they had heard all about Dottie's boyfriend Jim from home. Anyone who visited her dorm room gaped with undisguised envy at the strikingly handsome young man who was pictured in the framed photograph Dottie kept on her dresser.

Jim appeared to be an ardent suitor, writing Dottie regularly with news from home and telling her how much he missed her.

And it seemed to be a good match. She was the daughter of a Rear Admiral and Jim was a midshipman at the Naval Academy. Their futures were set —until the fall of their junior year when Jim wrote to tell her that he had fallen in love with someone else. Dottie was understandably shocked and devastated by the news.

When Christmas vacation came around, she felt relieved to be going home to get the support and love of her family and to see her high school pal, Buzz, who was now also at the Academy.

When the girls came back to Terrace House after the holidays, Dottie was her old, bubbly self again. What had happened over Christmas, they wondered?

Dottie kept her secret for a couple of days before she sat them down to relate what had transpired when she was home. As she explained, she and Buzz had gone out to dinner soon after she arrived as they normally did. During the meal, Dottie told Buzz how Jim had broken her heart by ending their engagement. Buzz had listened sympathetically, and then shocked her by confessing that he had been in love with her for years and was hoping that she could come to feel the same way about him some day.

It turned into a long evening of reminiscing over glasses of wine. As Dottie reflected with him on their times together, she realized how much Buzz had meant to her over the years, and that she did really love him.

During this narration, the four young women had sat transfixed, audibly sighing at the point where Dottie concluded that she was in love with Buzz. It was a such a romantic love story that they were left starry-eyed and elated about how things had turned out for their friend.

In the weeks that followed, Dottie was happier than ever and glowing with the certainty that she and Buzz had made a commitment to each other that would never be broken.

And she had been right. She and Buzz married the summer after graduation, stayed in Annapolis and started a family.

Alex couldn't wait to see her and hear about her life as a mother, a pre-school teacher, and a naval officer's wife.

She noticed then that she was coming into Montgomery and would need to start watching for I-65 which would take her directly to Mobile. She was less than 200 miles away from her destination.

As she merged left to join the southbound interstate, she cast her mind back to what she had been like in her school days. Unlike Josie and Dottie, she hadn't had any serious relationships. In fact, the only contact she had had with boys was at the occasional mixer when Woodley would invite nearby men's colleges like Lehigh or Johns Hopkins. Locally, there was Fort Detrick, the center for the U.S. biological weapons program, that would occasionally invite Woodley girls for parties. She always wondered what biological agents were being tested that week that might be in the punch.

Recalling herself as a student, Alex winced at the memory of her own poor study habits: skimming through daily assignments and then cramming for the tests; staying up half the night to type a term paper that was due the next day, still unsure whether the subject was appropriate – like when she made the poor choice of writing about the mafia as an urban problem for her Sociology term paper.

As an art major, she had been more interested in drawing and painting and had not concentrated enough on her academic courses, a failing she had regretted since then, ironically becoming more of a booklover since graduation.

***

The next two and a half hours passed slowly as signs of nearby cities disappeared, replaced by monotonous walls of scraggly southern loblolly and yellow pines lining both sides of the interstate. The exits that came up with regularity indicated few amenities for the traveler.

She had driven a third of the way down to Mobile before coming to an actual town. Greenville, with a population of just over 8,000, didn't hold much promise, either. Glancing at the blue services sign for food posted at Exit 130 as she sped past, she rejected the two she could read: The Bates House of Turkey and Bush's Bar-B-Que.

Alex shrugged and drove on, checking her GPS for how many more miles she had yet to go to reach her destination: 89. She sighed in resignation, thinking, *If this is the worst part of the week, I'll be lucky. I can manage going without lunch. I'm not sure how I'm going to manage dealing with an old friend who wants to knock off her cheating husband.*

Chapter 3

ALEX FELT A SENSE OF RELIEF driving on the bridge spanning the Mobile River, knowing she would soon be entering the city limits. Looking down, she thought how ironic it was that this sluggish olive-drab water would course its way south to join the cobalt waters of Mobile Bay and eventually mix in with the sparkling turquoise waters of the Gulf of Mexico.

Minutes later, the interstate became Water Street, the four-lane eastern boundary of the downtown historic district that ran alongside the river. It was a dowdy, colorless strip, characterized by low-roofed freight terminals and boxy pseudo-modern office buildings that were erected of poured concrete in the 1970s, a decade known for unimaginative architecture.

Alex looked around for any signs of Mardi Gras, but there was only the monotonous parade of commercial buildings concealing any signs of life.

Stopped at the light at St. Francis Street, her attention was drawn to a contemporary glass tower that rose above every other nearby structure. Peering up through the windshield, she followed the building's exterior to the top that boasted a graceful curved crown accentuated by a needle-like spire.

In the next block she came to Dauphin Street, the main east-west street in the historic district. Seeing the street sign, she had to say the name out loud, pronouncing it *Daw-feen',* which she knew was the French word for the oldest son of a king and heir to the throne.

Braking to a stop as the light turned red, she leaned over to look out the passenger window to get a better view of the street seeing colorful banners that had been stretched between light poles.

On the southwest corner, she observed an attractive old hotel constructed of ornamented cast iron. Arched windows with friezes in between were reminiscent of a Venetian palazzo.

Pulling ahead with traffic, she passed the sprawling convention center on her left just as the electronic voice in her GPS intoned that she should turn right in one tenth of a mile on Government Street. At that intersection, a regulatory road sign indicated that turning left would take her down into the Bankhead Tunnel that ran under the Mobile Bay, depositing cars on its eastern shore and to other towns.

She drove another five blocks and then turned left onto Claiborne Street. Then it was only one more block before the salmon pink Granada Inn came into view. Crossing Church Street, she turned into the Inn's adjacent parking lot and pulled into one of several empty spaces.

Grabbing her purse, she exited the car and stretched, turning her face to the sun, noting how mild the temperature was here, even at the end of February. Walking around to the back of the car, she hit the release on her remote to open the tailgate. Reaching in, she hauled out her suitcase and started on the short walk to the Inn. As she approached, she admired the hotel's Spanish American architecture.

Its former life as two separate, but identical, townhomes was apparent, despite the fact that they were now connected with a matching section. Enhancing the façade were balconies across both levels that were set off with ornamental black wrought-iron railings. On the ground level, a long dark green canopy led the way to the double front doors.

As she headed to the entrance, she felt more hopeful that Rosemary expected to fully enjoy the reunion as evidenced by her choice of this charming old hotel. It was right on the parade route and within walking distance to the Dauphin Street Historic District–which would put them in the middle of the celebration of Mardi Gras while getting reacquainted. She picked up her pace in anticipation of the upcoming visit with her old friends.

Chapter 4

ALEX PUSHED OPEN one of the dark green double doors with her suitcase and entered the lobby she found was unexpectedly bright and modern.

Setting down her luggage just inside, she checked her watch and discovered that she was an hour earlier than she had told Rosemary. Good. She'd have a little time to explore the hotel and get settled.

Looking across the lobby, a pair of glass-paned doors set in the center of a wall of long windows gave her a view of a large courtyard outside; a space that was walled off on the other three sides by two-story wings that had been built onto the original houses. At the center of the brick patio sat a large multi-tiered fountain set into a round basin. Scattered around the patio were several small ornamental trees boxed in by brick planters that overflowed with white and pink flowers.

The lobby itself was well-appointed with period furniture consisting of a Hepplewhite sofa and matching chairs flanked by mahogany tables. The arrangement contrasted with the more contemporary wall of windows across the back.

On her left, near the door, she examined the large oil portrait of a beautiful dark-haired woman dressed in a wedding gown from an earlier era.

"She's lovely, isn't she?"

Alex looked over in the direction of the voice, realizing it was the desk clerk who was addressing her. The middle-aged woman personified Southern style in her white bishop-sleeved blouse and chignon hair style.

Alex picked up her bag and crossed over to the desk. "She is. It's fine work, too. I went to art school so I was just studying the artist's technique that makes the woman look so life-like. Who is she?"

"She's one of the two sisters whose husbands built the original townhouses as wedding gifts. It was right during the Civil War." (She pronounced it as Civo Woah.)

Alex brightened. "Oh, yes, I read that on the website. I know this place remained in those two families for more than a hundred years. There must be a lot of stories about its past. I should explain that painting is a hobby of mine; I'm also self-employed as a tour operator, so I love coming upon treasures like this old inn."

The clerk smiled and nodded. "You've come to the right place, then. I could show you around a little if you have time. You *are* staying with us, aren't you?" She glanced down at Alex's suitcase.

"Oh, yes. Actually, there'll be three of us. A friend of ours from college lives in Mobile and picked this place for us for our own ten-year reunion." She glanced around as though they might have suddenly arrived. "My name is Alex Trotter. The other three are Dottie Byerly, Millie Townsend, and Josie Higgins."

The clerk brought up a screen on her computer and nodded. "Yes, I have the reservations. You're sharing rooms with two double-beds each, right?"

"Yes, that's what I understand. I'm probably the first one here."

"You're the first one to check in, I know. Actually, you're the first to check into the hotel today. I'm not even sure if your rooms are ready. Tell you what — since I'm not busy right now, how about if I show you around a little. Then you can explore on your own."

Alex nodded enthusiastically. "I'd love that . . . uh, Ms. Davis," she replied, squinting at the woman's name badge and seeing she was the manager.

"Call me Betsy. Well, good. You can leave your suitcase behind the desk here. I'll page my head housekeeper to keep a watch on the lobby for a bit."

After punching in numbers on her device, Betsy stood and pushed her chair aside to leave room for Alex to set her case down.

Within a minute or two, a thin, drawn woman appeared, carrying a clipboard. She was wearing a grey uniform and laced shoes. She glanced over at Alex, her face devoid of expression.

Betsy turned toward her. "Hi, Maria. Could you just stay around the lobby for a few minutes while I take Ms. Trotter on a short tour of the hotel?"

Maria nodded, unsmiling.

"Thanks. By the way, are the two double-bed rooms in the west townhouse made up yet? Ms. Trotter will be in one of them."

Maria looked down at her clipboard and ran a finger across. "*Sí.* Both are done."

"Good. Thanks, Maria. I'll be back in a few minutes. Just page me if you need me."

Betsy took Alex's arm and started toward the entryway. "We'll go out front, first." As they exited, she said in a low voice, "Poor Maria. She recently lost her daughter. She was Maria's whole world, too."

Alex frowned. "Oh, that's terrible. Was it an illness?"

"No. Honestly, it's a bit of a mystery. It appeared to have been an overdose, but I don't know and Maria doesn't talk about it. Carlotta was a lovely, sweet girl who had apparently gotten involved with the wrong crowd and started using drugs. It's just tragic. She was a real beauty, too." Betsy slowly shook her head.

Alex took a deep breath. "I'm really sorry to hear that."

Betsy put a hand on her arm. "Please don't say anything to Maria. She probably wouldn't want me to tell anyone."

"No, of course not."

"I just wanted to explain why she seems so sullen. Carlotta died only a week or so ago. Anyway, here's what I wanted to show you. The balcony right above us, outside Room 007, is where there have been sightings of the ghost of a young girl in a long white dress who paces back and forth."

Alex looked up at the balcony, wide-eyed. "Really? Why do they think her spirit is still here?"

"It's said that she still waits for her date for a Mardi Gras ball, but he never showed up. Someone else *did* . . . and murdered her."

Alex stiffened. "Oh, dear! Have you seen her ghost?"

Betsy nodded and sighed. "I've seen her—and the other ghosts, or at least evidence that they're here. Let's walk over to the west townhouse where you'll be staying."

Inside the front door, they walked past a staircase on their right and stopped in the hallway. Alex looked around at the few prints on the wallpaper and the runner on the old wood floor and then back at Betsy for an explanation.

Betsy smiled furtively. "You don't see anything unusual, do you? Watch this." She pushed on the dado rail and a doorway-sized opening was revealed that led into a narrow, low-ceilinged room.

"Oh, my gosh. You can't even see the seam in the wallpaper!" Alex exclaimed. "What is this?"

Betsy stepped inside and pulled up a trap door. "If we were to lower ourselves through this hole in the floor, we'd come to a room with an iron bed in it and further down we'd come into a tunnel. It's said that it was used to hide Confederate soldiers during the war."

Alex stepped inside to look down the hole. "Isn't that something? If I were in old clothes, I'd love to go down there."

Betsy replaced the cover. "If you want to see it sometime during your visit, I can have Maria take you down."

Back out in the hallway, Betsy dusted off her hands and led the way to the back and out into the courtyard.

Gesturing to the two and three-story additions, she said, "These were built in 1970 when the townhomes were sold by the descendants of the first families and the new owner converted the place into a hotel."

Alex looked up at numerous purple, gold and green banners festooning the space between columns on the balconies. "It's very festive out here."

Betsy opened the door to the lobby and waved to Maria at the desk. Seeing no one else in the area, she motioned to Alex to follow her to the doorway that led to the west townhouse. In the hallway, they again walked past the hidden panel and came to the staircase. Betsy started up the steps with Alex behind her.

"The room we're going to is just down the hall from yours," Betsy remarked as they continued climbing. "It's nice you're here and not in the new wing." She chuckled. "It's only fifty years old. In the South, that's still 'new,' y'know."

At the top of the stairs, they started down a long, carpeted hallway until they came to the third inset ivory door on their left. "Here we are." Betsy inserted a key card.

Alex peered into the room before she entered. "Do you see any spirits now?"

Betsy laughed. "Don't worry. Most of the ghosts in this place remain unseen. They just unplug lamps and move beds and things."

"Oh, that's a big comfort," Alex said, rolling her eyes.

In the center of the room hung a large beaded mushroom-shaped chandelier. Betsy pointed up at it. "This is the light fixture that sways when Mz. Sinclair is fussin' about something."

Alex stared at it for several seconds as though it might start swinging. Looking back at Betsy she asked, "Do you charge less for this room?"

"Oh, I think we should charge mo-ah," Betsy answered with an exaggerated accent.

They both laughed.

"Well, maybe you want to get back to the lobby to collect your case and wait for your friend," Betsy said, turning off a lamp on the nightstand. "Oh, by the way, this phone sometimes rings when there's no one on the other end. It's said that it's one of the sister brides calling the other who used to have this room."

Alex made a show of heading toward the door. "Okay. That's it. Enough ghosts. Anyway, this all reminds me that I told my husband I'd call him as soon as I arrived to assure him I was safe and sound. He should know that the only scary people here have been dead for a hundred years."

Chapter 5

ALEX CHUCKLED TO herself as she ended her cell phone call with Arlie. He had been amused by her stories of the haunting of the Granada Inn, being totally skeptical of the existence of ghosts. He had wondered what people could do on Halloween if ghosts are running around all the time, anyway. Alex thought the legend of the ghosts added to the ambience of the place, even if they were figments of people's imaginations.

Setting down her phone, she looked around at the period-styled room with its flocked red wallpaper and antique four poster beds, appreciating the effort that had been made to retain an 18th century ambience in the townhouses. Long pleated draperies flanked the two large double-hung windows that allowed muted light to enter while affording a full view of the courtyard below.

Opening her suitcase on the bed, she lifted her navy-blue gown out and hung it in the wardrobe along with a couple of blouses and a jacket. After she placed her folded clothes in one of the drawers of the bow-front dresser, she sank down in one of the wing chairs to rest. Closing her eyes, she thought about all that the people who had lived in this house had been through. Having read up on the area before her visit, she could imagine the terror the young newlyweds must have felt as Civil War battles broke out within a few miles of here. The tide of the war had turned to the advantage of the North in 1864 when Confederate gunboats in Mobile Bay were overwhelmed by the Union Navy led by Admiral David Farragut. This was the battle where it was alleged he uttered his famous line, "Damn the torpedoes, full speed ahead!" in securing the victory.

The next year, three days after the surrender of Robert E. Lee at Appomattox, the city of Mobile surrendered to the Union army to avoid further destruction.

Alex thought about how the townhouses had been home for so many succeeding generations of those original families and, since the sale and the additions built on, they had served as a hotel for another fifty years. She'd have to explore more of the Inn. Maye she'd ask to be taken down to the tunnel under the houses.

Her reverie was interrupted with the shrill ringing of the room phone. Looking over at the outdated instrument on the nightstand, she thought it might be the ghost of one of the sister brides calling. Getting to her feet, she picked up the receiver on the third ring and heard a live person on the other end.

"Hi, Ms. Trotter. It's Betsy at reception. Your friend, Rosemary Stuart, is here. She wants to know if she should come up or if you'd like to come down."

"Tell her I'll be right down. I want to show her around a little. Thanks."

Alex checked herself in the oval dresser mirror. Digging in her purse, she took out a lipstick and a hairbrush. After making a few touch-ups, she patted down her fine wavy auburn hair that had frizzed up in the humidity, and made a face in the mirror. *Rosemary will recognize me with my unruly hair, anyway.*

Quickly making her way along the corridor, she bounded down the stairs and then the hallway that led to the lobby door.

As she walked in, she saw Rosemary sitting demurely on the Hepplewhite sofa gazing out the front windows.

"Rosemary!" Alex called out.

Rosemary turned, her face brightening with a wide grin. "Alex!" she answered, jumping to her feet and crossing the room to hug her friend.

"You look great!" the women said in unison and then laughed.

Alex held Rosemary at arm's length. "Seriously, you look just like you did on graduation day."

"That bad, huh."

Alex playfully gave her a shake. "You're funny. Let's find a place to sit and catch up for a bit and then look around the hotel. Have you heard from the others?"

"They wrote me with their flights." She looked down at her watch. "Let's see. It's a little after two. From the arrival times they gave me, they were close enough that they should be on the same shuttle from the airport. Betsy told me the next one would be leaving at two-thirty and it's a half-hour drive here."

"Okay, perfect. That gives us some time to talk. I wonder if there's a small lounge …" she turned toward the reception desk. "Betsy?"

The desk clerk looked up from her paperwork. "Yes, Ms. Trotter?"

"Is there a sitting room where we could talk?"

"Sure. The lounge in the east townhouse, right through that doorway and down the hall. Y'all should be alone there now."

A minute later the two women were seated across from each other in the loveseats that flanked a stone fireplace. Alex leaned back against the cushion and took a breath. "It's so great to see you, and I love this place you found for us. It just reeks of history. Did you know it's haunted?"

Rosemary made a guttural sound. "Please. Places all over Mobile claim to be haunted. They should rename the place Amityville."

"Hah!" Alex barked. "You should have Betsy give you the tour. You'll see the Inn is pretty spooky. I've read reviews by guests who said their furniture was moved and lamps were unplugged during the night. One said she felt someone get in bed with her when she was alone."

Rosemary made a face. "That was probably Mitch."

Alex snickered then covered her mouth. "I shouldn't laugh at that. What's the latest with him? Have you been able to find out for sure if he's having an affair?"

"No. You discouraged me from espionage. Besides, I don't need to prove it to know it. He comes and goes as he pleases. Our love life is practically non-existent. He's taken a couple of 'fishing trips' when he didn't come back with any fish. Shall I go on?"

"So, what are you going to do about it? Get a divorce?"

"I can't."

"Why not?"

"Are you kidding? He's the county District Attorney. He'd probably get an order for me to pay *him* alimony from my poor little job at the school. We don't have children, so I'm on my own."

"Well, you can't kill him."

"I *could.* I make most of his food and I can get anti-freeze."

"Rosemary!"

"Oh, don't get excited. I'm not going to kill the man. Not that I haven't thought about it, but I'm not capable. My life isn't totally miserable, anyway. We have some good times. Mitch is still charming when he wants to be. By the way, he wants to meet all of you while you're here."

Alex's hands flew up. "Oh, that reminds me! Betsy told me you 'Goddesses' are having your ball here Tuesday night. The courtyard's perfect for that, not to mention the convenience for us. Mitch'll be coming to that, right?"

"He'll be there. He told me this morning he's going as Robert the Bruce. Y'now, Braveheart. I think he just wants to wear a kilt. Anyway, he asked if we could all meet for a drink before that. You can't really have a conversation at one of these Mardi Gras balls."

"Oh, sure, fine.-If that's what you want."

They both looked toward the doorway, seeing the housekeeper with a basket of bottles and cloths standing there uncertainly. "Maria, did you want to get in here?" Alex asked.

"*Desculpe, señoras*. I, uh, just want to dust the furniture. *Dos minutos*." She held up two fingers.

Alex looked over at Rosemary who checked her watch. "The others should be here soon. And you said you want to show me around first."

"Right. Let's go and let Maria do her work. I can't wait to see everyone. This will be the best time we've ever had together."

Chapter 6

"WE SHOULD GO DOWN here," Alex advised as she held up the trap door in the hidden room.

Rosemary wrinkled her nose. "Why would we want to do that? This place is creepy enough without going down to the bunkers like a couple of Nazis."

"Oh, you're no fun. I'm going to ask Maria to take me down—maybe tomorrow. This is real-life history going back like a hundred and fifty years."

"I'm happy for you. Let's go out in the courtyard. I want to see what we still need to have people set up for Tuesday night. Also, I want to check out the bar in the Carriage House. I'm pretty sure we'll need an outside bar, too."

Alex dropped the trapdoor and wiped her hands on her slacks. "Okay. Good idea. Then we should go look for the others."

Crossing to the other side of the courtyard, they came to the former Carriage House, lifted the latch on the plank door, and pushed it open. Inside, they found themselves in a brick-walled room, softly lit by wrought-iron lanterns that hung along the walls between pub tables. The L-shaped bar had a thick wood top coated in glossy varnish. Above the bar, wine glasses were hung between wood strips. Behind the bar, a wall of shelving was filled with liquor bottles.

Rosemary looked around, nodding approvingly. "See how nice this is? Much more inviting than a tunnel."

'This *is* nice, "Alex agreed. "We should all have a glass of wine here before we go out tonight. It's still early so we can probably have the place to ourselves."

Rosemary held up her watch. "They should be walking in any minute. Let's go check the lobby."

A half hour later, Rosemary, Alex, and the three recent arrivals were seated at one of the tables in the Carriage House. The only other patrons, two middle-aged men at the bar, gazed admiringly at the five attractive women.

"I can't get over that we're finally back together after so many years," Dottie enthused, her gaze taking in every one at the table.

Alex noted her friend's still fair complexion and very fine, light brown hair, recalling Dottie joking that she had only three hairs on her head. What people noticed were her twinkling blue eyes and ready smile.

Millie was sitting quietly with her chin resting on her clasped hands, her intelligent brown eyes surveying the group. "We're not 'just like we were'," she argued. "Back then, we were carefree students. Now, you and Josie are mothers and teachers, Rosemary is a school counselor and married to the county D.A., and Alex and I have travelled the world in our careers."

Josie twisted her mouth. "Hmm. The three of us sound kinda dull in comparison to you and Alex."

"Yeah, thanks," Rosemary agreed.

Millie shook her head. "I didn't mean that at all. I meant that we've all gone in different directions since school, and yet we still have a lot in common."

Josie looked sideways at her. "Nice save. I'll accept that. So, you and Alex should compare notes on your travels. You've probably been to a lot of the same places."

Millie sniggered. "I don't think Alex has taken one of her tour groups to Afghanistan." Looking off into space, she continued, dramatically, "I can see the itinerary now: 'Day one: Bone-rattling ride in jeeps through the scorching desert outside Kabul. If we don't run into a landmine, an insurgent attack, or an IED, we'll be around for dinner consisting of goat kebabs served under a tent. Remember, no liquor allowed—under pain of death. Day two: Leave for Turkey . . . or anywhere else that is better than this."

Alex laughed along with the others. "That's pretty good. I should tell you I had enough trouble on a Rhine River cruise with a few senior citizens who weren't actual terrorists; but thanks for the advice about tours in war zones."

"What went wrong on your cruise?" Dottie asked.

Alex murmured she'd tell her later as Rosemary raised her index finger to get everyone's attention. "We need to talk about the events over the next two days. If you want to see the Neptune's Daughters' parade tonight, it's at six forty-five. It'll be going down Government Street where we can get something to eat, too. They'll have lots of decorative floats and jazz bands. Does that sound good?"

"Sure," Josie answered. "You're in charge. You just tell us what we're doing when, and we'll go along, right?" She looked around at the others who nodded and gave their approval.

"Okay, good," Rosemary said. "I thought tomorrow we'd just bum around and go to some of the tourist places like the Carnival Museum where they have the lavish costumes of former Mardi Gras Kings and Queens. Then, there's an antebellum plantation, and a couple Victorian homes open to the public. Things like that."

"Sounds better than Millie's tour of Kabul," Alex quipped.

Rosemary gave a little snort. "I would hope so. Anyway, tomorrow evening I thought we'd meet Mitch for drinks . . . if he doesn't have a date."

"What?!" Dottie and Josie said in unison.

Rosemary flipped a hand in the air. "Forget I said that. I'm sure Mitch will be on his best behavior tomorrow night. Anyway, after drinks, I'm thinking we'll have dinner at one of the nicer seafood restaurants for our big night out."

"Sounds wonderful," Dottie commented. "I bet they have great seafood here. In Annapolis you can get any kind of fish you like — as long as it's bass. Anyway, tell us more about Tuesday night's shindig for all of you Goddesses. What are you going as?"

Rosemary clasped her hands together, her gray-green eyes brightening. "I think I came up with a perfect costume. Tell me what you think. I'm going to go as . . . Mary, Queen of Scots. Get it? She was Mary Stuart, and I'm Rosemary Stuart. And I'm Scottish, too."

Everyone complimented her, agreeing it was a clever idea.

"Are you sure we can't wear costumes, too?" Millie asked.

"No, it's prohibited if you're not a Goddess." Rosemary's face crinkled in amusement. "I know it sounds ridiculous, but Mobile takes this Mardi Gras business seriously. You all brought long dresses, didn't you? They're like mandatory for guests."

"I have a long skirt and top," Josie said. "Nothing too fancy. What did you bring, Alex?"

"My pink bridesmaid dress from your wedding."

Josie's mouth dropped open. "Really?"

"No. . . not really." Alex grinned at her. "Not that I don't like it, but it's hardly a versatile dress, you have to admit."

Dottie chuckled. "Josie and I got married when fairytale weddings were 'in.' I think brides now are more practical."

"By the time I get married you'll all be in pantsuits," Millie declared.

Rosemary tapped on her watch as the others scoffed at Millie's forecast. "We should get going now if we don't want to miss any of the Daughters of Neptune. We'll have a lot more time to talk."

"The Mystic Goddess has spoken," Millie deadpanned as they started pushing back their chairs. "And I for one don't want to see what happens if we disobey her."

Chapter 7

LATER THAT EVENING, the five friends stood together behind the crowd-control barriers waving, clapping, and cheering along with thousands of others along the parade route in the Historic District.

During the past two hours they had seen a dozen tiered floats pass by, all elaborately decorated in an aquatic motif to honor Neptune, the Roman god of the sea.

Rosemary told them that the floats had been constructed over a period of months; that the different decks were first built over a base platform and then set off by the low walls painted in colorful designs or scenes. Most of the floats featured large fixed or animated figures that had been modeled out of wire mesh covered with a wet plastic compound that would dry smooth and hard, ready for decorating. The portable generators onboard provided electricity for the recorded music and the multiple strings of twinkling lights.

The men and women on the floats were dressed in elaborate costumes~~,~~ and threw beaded necklaces, trinkets, and stuffed toys to the onlookers, as well as frequently showering them with handfuls of glitter as they passed by.

"What kind of cookies or cakes are these?" Dottie shouted, having snatched a couple of the cellophane-wrapped treats out of the air.

"They're Moon Pies," Rosemary yelled back. "They've been around for a hundred years."

"Not these, I hope," Dottie said, snickering. "Are they good?"

Rosemary made a face. "Of course, they're good. They're graham cracker cookies filled with marshmallow and dipped in chocolate. How bad can they be? Grab as many as you can for all of us."

Millie jumped up and hauled in another beaded necklace, pulling it over her head to add to her collection. "Jeez. I love these!"

Rosemary glanced over at her. "You don't ever wear jewelry. Now, suddenly, you're Cleopatra."

The rumbling of engines signaled a company of motorcycles approaching with purple, green and gold streamers flying from their handlebars. On the closest bike, a small white dog~~,~~ wearing a pink cape, sat on the raised cushion behind the driver. Alex pointed to the dog and said to Josie, "I've heard that's called the bitch seat, so the dog sitting there makes perfect sense."

The next float caught everyone's attention with its bevy of over-sized bare-chested female figures up front, their bottom halves covered with panels with tops sculpted into waves and painted in shades of turquoise and blue. They continued along the sides of the float and across the back. On an huge throne atop the float sat a super-sized green King Neptune, complete with a trident, crown on his head, and lightning bolts coming out of his fingers. Human-like daughters of Neptune, dressed as mermaids, were curled up on cushions, seductively waving to the crowds while young men in pirate costumes stood on the float's platform and threw beaded necklaces. Reggae music blared from the back of the rig.

That exhibit was followed by a couple dozen clomping horses being ridden by men dressed in tricked-out Revolutionary War uniforms complete with tri-cornered hats and navy jackets decorated with gold epaulets and brass buttons.

"I wonder why they don't use Confederate soldier uniforms?" Dottie said.

Rosemary shrugged, "Probably because the Revolutionary War had cooler outfits. Grey uniforms and squashed hats don't have the same panache."

At that point the metallic, bright notes of a brass band were heard playing "When the Saints go Marching In." After the first verse, the song was transposed to a higher key, adding even more energy to the tune.

Rosemary nudged Josie. "I bet the band stops playing *right* before they get here. That always happens."

Josie patted her on the shoulder. "I'm sure we'll hear that song often enough."

Several minutes later, the band stopped in front of them, still playing "Saints" with the horn players making a show of moving their instruments up and down with the beat. The crowd joined in by singing, swaying, and prancing around to the music.

The band played through the verse one more time, and then struck up "Mardi Gras in Mobile" featuring the saxophones. After several bars, the musicians started back down the parade route.

"So, did you get enough of 'The Saints go Marching In'?" Josie asked Rosemary.

"That should hold me 'til the next funeral." She agreed. "That reminds me; they would have sounded great on 'Nearer my God to Thee,' too, but that seems to be the end of the parade. Here comes the street cleaner."

"I don't think it's possible to get rid of all this glitter," Alex commented, kicking up a pile of the stuff.

"They can't. I've heard there are a hundred pounds on each float. You'll find that the streets and sidewalks always sparkle a little here. The rest sinks into the ground, I guess."

Right then Josie called out, "So, should we go back to the inn?"

Everyone agreed they had had enough excitement for one day, and started making their way through the crowd to walk the six blocks back to the Granada. As they crossed the street at the intersection, Rosemary grabbed Alex by the arm. "Holy crap! I can't believe that—that SOB."

Alex scanned the thinning crowd where she was pointing. "Who?"

Rosemary's finger was shaking. "The dark-haired man in the camel jacket walking with the redhead. That's Mitch."

Alex nodded. "Oh . . . I see them. Do you know her?"

"Of course not," Rosemary snapped. "He told me he was working late on a case. Then he'd grab something downtown. Looks like that's what he grabbed."

Alex winced. "Uh, could she be a lawyer?"

Rosemary glared at her. "Does she *look* like a lawyer? Did you ever see a lawyer with that much makeup or with hair that bright? She looks more like someone who *needs* a lawyer."

Alex checked her laugh. "Stay with that thought. She doesn't look like someone who would be in a serious relationship with any husband of yours."

"Well, she's holding onto his arm. That suggests an intimacy to me."

Alex bit down on her lip. "I know it looks bad. I'm just saying that Mitch might have a good explanation."

Rosemary snorted. "Well, I can tell you this; if he doesn't have one, he can sure as hell make one up."

Alex held up her hands in surrender. "Okay. I'm just saying it's possible she could be someone he ran into who he's helped out in his position."

"Alex, he's a prosecutor, not a Public Defender. He doesn't *help* people in his position."

"All right. All right. Maybe the woman works in his office. You don't know. How about you mention, just off-handedly, that you saw him tonight after the parade and see what he says. Then take it from there. I mean, why make yourself crazy at this point?"

"*Off-handedly,*" Rosemary mocked. "Hah! Yeah, I'll just say, off-handedly, 'I saw you with your latest bimbo. Is that the best you can do?'"

Alex sighed audibly.

"Okay. I won't say that—exactly. I don't think I can be as casual as you'd like, but I won't throw a frying pan at him, either. I want to keep the peace while you all are in town."

Alex gave her a squeeze. "Good. Remember, you hold the cards; he has to make the next play. Let's catch up with the others. We can sit around at the Granada and talk for a while before you go home."

"Right. I'll blow off a little steam with them, too. Josie will have some sensible advice; Millie will tell me to shoot him in the groin; and Dottie will tell me how I deserve much better. Yeah, it'll help to talk to them."

Alex nudged her. "Hopefully, you can work it out somehow with Mitch before tomorrow night when we're all supposed to be getting together. We shouldn't let on you told us what you saw tonight. I'd like to see what the guy is like without that tension. Actually, I'm looking forward to meeting him after all I've heard. But I want things to work out best for you."

Rosemary smiled wanly. "Thanks. I'm glad you and the others are here. And I promise I won't spoil your visit. We'll have fun tomorrow doing the tourist things and then have a nice dinner. If Mitch shows up, it'll be because we've reached some kind of truce for the time being."

Chapter 8

THE NEXT MORNING Alex woke up early with an uneasy feeling about how the day would go. The night before, Rosemary had become even more upset when she told the others about seeing her husband with another woman. Sympathizing with their friend, the other three had agreed with Rosemary's interpretation of the situation which had probably only fueled her outrage.

Alex had seen Rosemary's temper often enough to worry about what she might do. By the time Rosemary left, Alex found herself feeling sorry for Mitch.

Now, she sat up in bed to contemplate getting up. The room was dark and quiet. Glancing across to the other bed, she saw that Josie appeared to be still sleeping. Checking the clock on the nightstand, she saw it was 6:50, a little early to get up considering they didn't expect Rosemary until ten. Before that, they only had to shower, dress, and have some breakfast downstairs.

However, she was too unnerved to go back to sleep, so she might as well use the bathroom first and get dressed. By the time she was finished getting ready, Josie would probably be getting up.

An hour later, Alex was sitting in one of the wing chairs checking her emails and phone messages while Josie was getting dressed. There was nothing from Rosemary, which was good—she hoped. Of course, it was still early. She couldn't stop wondering about how it went last night and what Rosemary's mood was like today, and whether they were still planning to meet Mitch for drinks and dinner.

"Hear anything from Rosemary?" Josie asked, coming out of the bathroom, freshly made-up and smartly dressed in checked jacket, turtleneck, and slacks.

"Hah! You're worried, too? No, there's nothing. I was just thinking I'd send her a message to confirm we'll be ready by ten, if not before, as we're about to go down for breakfast. She'll probably respond and then we'd get some sense of how things stand. What do you think?"

Josie nodded. "Sure. Can't hurt. Should we call Dottie and Millie? See if they're ready?"

"They said they'd plan on breakfast at eight thirty, so we have a few minutes. I'll write this note and send it off and then maybe we can walk around the courtyard before breakfast. They've put up more decorations."

A minute later there was a knock on the door. Josie went to look through the peephole before opening it.

"Hi. You guys ready?" Millie said, entering just ahead of Dottie. "We figured you were probably up early, too."

Josie closed the door behind them. "All set. Alex is just sending Rosemary a note to confirm our plans for this morning."

Millie's eyes sparkled, impishly. "And to find out what kind of mood she's in."

"Oh, she'll be fine with us," Dottie put in. "She's matured over the last ten years— like we all have."

Alex rose from her chair and walked over to the dresser to pick up her purse. "Let's put it out of our minds for now and just enjoy our breakfast. We'll see her in a couple of hours and find out what's what."

Downstairs, they opened the door into the lobby and entered. Behind the desk, Betsy looked up and smiled. "Hi, ladies. How do y'all like your rooms?"

"Oh, they're great," Dottie enthused. "We love the antique pieces."

"I'm glad. Y'all are in for a real treat tomorrow night. We'll be setting up the courtyard today and tomorrow. It'll look like a fairyland."

"We're excited about that," Josie said. "This is the first Mardi-Gras for all of us."

"Well, you came to the right one. Most people don't know when it comes to celebrating Mardi-Gras, we have it all over Nawlins."

"New Orleans," Alex said under her breath to the other three.

Leaving the lobby, they walked down the hallway until they came to the paneled, wainscoted dining room, across from the sitting room, and found an available table by a window. Alex hung her purse over the back of one of the chairs to reserve it while they served themselves at the buffet table.

"I'm going to have just a beignet, fruit and coffee," Alex said.

"Ben what?" Dottie asked, picking up a plate.

"*Ben-yays.* Beignets are like square donuts, but lighter and with powdered sugar on top. There's a case of them under a heat lamp over there to keep them hot."

"Oh—like Krispy Kremes," Millie said with a wink.

Alex gave her a look. "Not exactly. By the way, the coffee here's a little different, too. It has chicory in it. If you haven't had that, it has a nutty flavor. I think you'll like it."

At ten o'clock, the four of them stood out in front of the Inn, craning their necks to look past the parked cars to see if Rosemary was coming.

Millie moved forward a couple steps to get a better view. "There's no sign of her."

"I'm surprised she's not here, yet," Dottie said, looking at her watch. "She's never late."

"Oh, don't worry," Alex said. "As I told you, she sounded fine in her message. She's probably looking for a parking space. We'll be walking over to visit the Carnival Museum."

Josie pointed down the street. "I think that's her now."

The four stared as the black Honda was backed into a parking space across the street. Seeing Rosemary exit the vehicle, smile and wave, all four exhaled in unison.

"See, we had nothing to worry about," Dottie said.

Millie elbowed her. "*You* were the one who was worried. Anyway, Rosemary looks like her same, sweet self. Love that cape she's wearing."

Rosemary started across the street toward them. Alex had to agree she looked like her normal pretty self: wavy, chestnut hair that curled under just so, luminous hazel eyes, and a smile that brought out her dimples.

"I hope I'm not late," Rosemary said as she walked up, noting their relieved looks.

"Oh, no," Josie said. "Not at all. We just came out a little early. Looking forward to having you show us Mobile."

Alex tapped her index finger on her lips. "Uh — before we get going, to be honest, we were wondering if we're still meeting Mitch for drinks later."

Rosemary pushed her hair behind one ear and pressed her lips together for a moment. "Yes, he'll meet us at one of the bars in the Historic District at five. I know you want to hear what he had to say for himself when I told him I saw him with another woman — and I'll tell you all about it, but I'll save that for lunch. I think you'll be surprised by what he had to say. I know I was. One thing about Mitch—he has an answer for everything."

Chapter 9

IT WAS AN EASY TWO-BLOCK walk to the restored Victorian mansion that housed the Carnival Museum.

Entering through the double doors on the wide front porch, they were greeted by a young man with a ready smile and a name tag that read, 'Stephen.'

"Good morning, ladies. Welcome to the Carnival Museum. Is this your first time with us?"

Four of them nodded as Millie spoke up. "It's our first time in Mobile. We're visiting our friend, here."

"I see. Well, thanks for coming. You can buy tickets from our cashier over there, but first let me give you a little history so you can better appreciate the collection."

"That'd be great. Thanks," Dottie said.

"No problem. Well, we're proud that Mobile was the first place in the country to commemorate Mardi Gras, in 1703. Our first masked society was founded in 1830. There are now about sixty societies who celebrate with parades and balls for three weeks every February." He paused to gather his thoughts.

"We've heard of the societies," Millie said. "Our friend, here, is a Mystic Goddess."

Rosemary blushed as Stephen turned his attention to her. "Oh, really. Have you ever been the queen?"

"Uh, yes. Two years ago, with my husband as the king. It was a lot of fun."

"I'm sure," Stephen agreed.

Millie patted Rosemary's shoulder. "She's going to the ball tomorrow night as a queen—Mary Stuart."

Rosemary waved away the remark. "My costume is *nothing* like the elaborate costumes the society queens wear."

Stephen gestured toward the interior of the museum. "You'll see what she means with the extensive collection of king and queen costumes we have inside that go back to 1921. Just take your time and look around. Any questions right now?"

They all shook their heads.

"Well, if you think of something, there are attendants throughout the museum. Okay? Enjoy."

They all murmured their thanks as they started towards the cashier to buy their tickets for admission.

Once inside, they roamed from room to room marveling at the displays that were set out on raised platforms, each one comprised of a male and female mannequin wearing the costumes of a particular king and queen. The male figure was dressed in either a period military uniform, an embroidered tunic, or an Eastern caftan. The female figure was always dressed in a lavishly decorated ball gown. The sets of mannequins all wore crowns inset with costume emeralds, rubies, and diamonds. What were referred to as 'robes' were actually ten to twenty-foot trains dramatically laid out on an incline facing the visitors. The trains were always made out of a rich fabric, like a heavy velvet, and edged in ermine or some other exotic fur. The body of the trains featured bold designs outlined in gold braiding and encrusted with sequins and jewels.

As the group paused by one female mannequin dressed in an elegant beige silk and lace gown, Millie commented, "Can you imagine Queen Elizabeth in something like that? With all her money she wears those frumpy jacket dresses with unflattering round-brimmed hats."

Josie chuckled. "She's frugal and likes to be comfortable. That's veddy British."

After about an hour they exited the museum, waving to Stephen as he was giving his spiel to a middle-aged couple.

Outside, they started back to the inn, chatting about what they had seen. Alex came up alongside Rosemary and elbowed her. "So — should we go to lunch now?"

Rosemary turned to look at her. "I know you want to hear about Mitch, but it's not even noon yet.

I thought we'd visit the Bragg-Mitchell mansion first; then eat. It won't take more than an hour for that. We can all squeeze into my car to drive over and then go to lunch in the area."

Twenty minutes later they were driving up a long, winding, pea-gravel drive, approaching the Greek Revival and Italianate antebellum plantation. The front of the white-frame building boasted a wide deep porch that went around the sides of the house and was accented with two-story pillars.

After parking in the visitors' lot in back, they exited the car and started up the path that led to the front of the house. As they came around the corner, Rosemary gestured broadly across the property. "See all those giant live oaks in the yard? The original trees were cut down to give the Confederate army room to shell the Union troops. Wasn't that considerate of the plantation owner? He was a judge named Bragg. After the war, he replanted the trees using acorns from the original oaks, which is pretty neat."

They stood gazing across the property for a minute, trying to imagine the place during and right after the Civil War.

Josie tapped her finger on her mouth, thinking. "Considering that the owner was a judge and owned this large estate, he was probably at least forty at the time; and since the average lifespan then was about 50, he couldn't have lived long enough to see his acorns become trees."

Millie gave a little snort. "Leave it to Josie to figure *that* out. I liked thinking that the poor guy saw his plantation restored after he destroyed the place for a war that the South ended up losing."

Rosemary turned toward the house and waved them on to follow her. "Let's go inside. I don't think you'll feel sorry for the judge when you see how he lived. Besides, it could be just a legend about the trees."

They spent the next forty-five minutes on a guided tour of the home that had been restored by the Mitchell family and donated to the city. Each room had been elegantly decorated and furnished with pieces in the styles of the late 19th century.

When they were finished with their tour, Rosemary led the way out the back door. "We'll go to lunch now, if all of you are ready."

Twenty minutes later, they were sitting at a table in a casual restaurant located on the main road back to the Granada Inn.

After ordering their sandwiches and salads, Alex nudged Rosemary seated next to her. "I don't want to rush you, but any time you're ready to tell us what your husband had to say for himself, we're ready to listen."

"All right, all right. Let me think about it for a minute."

Dottie smoothed her napkin on her lap. "You don't have to tell us if you don't want to."

"Yes, she does," Millie said. "We're all interested in his explanation — for her sake. And by 'we,' I mean 'me'."

Rosemary snickered. "Same old Millie. Always speaks her mind. Okay, here's what happened last night. When I got home, I was surprised to find that Mitch was even there. And then, he seemed like his normal self. He was watching the late news and looked relaxed. I told him we needed to talk and he turned down the volume and calmly looked at me, waiting. I kept my voice low when I told him I had seen him with a red-haired woman after the parade and I wondered who she was and why she was with him, holding onto his arm.

"He rubbed his forehead like he was trying to remember. Then he said, and I quote, 'Oh, maybe that was Stacy Gibson.' I said, 'How many red-haired women were you with tonight?' He gave a little laugh, then said that she's a prostitute, like he had said, 'she's a secretary.' I'm sure I looked shocked because he quickly added that she was a defendant he had helped out as D.A. According to Mitch, she had been picked up for solicitation and met with him to beg him not to send her to jail, that she would lose the job she had just started as a hotel maid; that she had quit turning tricks and had entered a rehab program. He said he verified her employment, and thought she deserved a break, so he dropped the charges. During the parade he stopped at an oyster bar to get something to eat and ran into her when he came out. She thanked him again for his help. He didn't remember that she had held onto his arm."

Rosemary looked around at the stunned faces. "So . . . that's it."

"Wow," Alex said. "I thought I was reaching when I suggested she was someone he had helped in court. Sounds like you believe him, right?"

Rosemary shrugged. "I guess so. I mean, he didn't stumble around coming up with a story, and it *is* plausible. Honorable, even."

Millie puckered her lips in thought. "You know, he might have seen you at the parade and worked out what he would say in case you had seen him, too."

"Hmm. I hadn't thought about that. He could just as well have seen me. Anyway, at this point, I'll take him at his word. If he made it up, I have to give him credit for coming up with a good explanation for being with a prostitute, I guess." She rolled her eyes. "Anyway, I don't want to spend any more time talking about Mitch while you're here. I want to hear about your families and what you've been up to. And tomorrow night we'll all enjoy the ball."

Chapter 10

AS ALEX PUSHED OPEN THE DOOR to the bistro, the room was pulsating to the beat of an island song that was a popular Mardi Gras anthem. The recording featured a male lead with an echoing chorus:

"Talk-in' 'bout, Hey now! Hey now!
Hey now! I-ko, I-ko, unday!
Jock-a-mo fee-no ai na-né,
Jock-a-mo fee na-né."

The din of conversation mixed in with the music as waitresses, balancing trays full of drinks, circulated around the boisterous crowd.

The four women stood peering into the darkness trying to spot Rosemary. Millie swayed to the music.

After a minute, the man standing next to the hostess approached.

"Hi, ladies. Welcome to Cyril's. Do you need a table?"

Alex shook her head. "We're looking for a friend who should be here already."

He nodded. "Feel free to walk back to take a better look. I like to keep the lighting cut back to make the place cozy. I'm Cyril Green, the owner, by the way."

Alex smiled as she glanced around. "I like the atmosphere — the strings of colored lights around the room . . . and the music. It's all good."

Green nodded. "Thanks. Your first time here?"

"Yes. We're visiting a friend. We're from out of town."

"There she is, in the back!" Dottie called out, waving.

Alex nodded to the owner. "Seems we've spotted her. Nice to meet you. See you later."

"Oh, oh. It looks like she's alone," Dottie added, under her breath.

Josie checked her watch. "It's just five o'clock. She said Mitch would be coming from the office, so he's probably just not here yet."

"Well, let's go back and find out," Alex suggested, leading the way.

As they approached her table, Rosemary smiled and fluttered her fingers from where she sat at one end. The four of them chose seats on the sides, leaving the other end chair unoccupied.

"Is Mitch coming?" Millie asked as she sat down.

"Yeah, sure. He should be here shortly. He was planning on leaving work at five. I don't know why he wasn't keen about meeting here, but it seemed to me to be the best place for us. It's just a block from where we're going to have dinner. Oh, here comes the waitress . . . again. She keeps checking with me to see if I want to order something. Jeez, do I look like I want to drink alone? I came early to be sure we got a table for six."

The thin, middle-aged woman approached with an order pad in hand. "Hi, ladies," she said in the raspy voice of a smoker. "I'm Shirley and I'll be your server. Is everyone here now?"

Rosemary answered, "No, we're expecting one more — but we can order-drinks now."

"Did you need menus, or is it just drinks tonight?"

"I think we'll just be ordering just drinks . . . unless someone wants an appetizer?" Rosemary glanced around at the others.

"Not for me, thanks," Millie answered as the others shook their heads.

"Well, I'll start," Rosemary said. "I'd like a glass of your house Chardonnay."

The others followed with their drink orders that Shirley noted on her pad. 'Okay, thanks. I'll be right back with these."

As she walked away, Rosemary leaned forward on her elbows with her hands clasped. "This should be an interesting evening. By the way, I told Mitch that I didn't mention that Stacy woman to you all."

Millie gave Rosemary a look. "Yeah, I'm sure he believes that."

Rosemary shrugged. "Well, anyway, it takes that subject off the table." Her attention became drawn to the front door. "Well, speak of the devil; here he comes now."

The others turned in their seats to look towards the front of the bar. The lanky, dark-haired man who Alex recognized seemed to be engaged in a heated conversation with Cyril Green, repeatedly jabbing the man in the chest. Green backed away, shaking his head. After a few seconds, Mitch turned and started walking in their direction.

Halfway back, one of the waitresses tugged at his sleeve to say something in his ear. He then straightened and spoke out of the side of his mouth without looking at her, and kept walking.

As he caught Rosemary's eye, he raised his chin to acknowledge her. As he walked up, he gave her a peck on the forehead.

Rosemary held onto his jacket sleeve. "What was that about — at the door?"

"Huh? Oh, that guy's the owner. I just let him know there are some kids blocking the front door and being loud and obnoxious. There's another damn parade coming, so it's like a zoo out there."

Rosemary twisted her mouth. "Well, you got through it, so that's good. You're at the end, there."

He walked around the table and pulled out his chair. As he was lowering himself, he flashed a broad smile at the other four women. "Sorry I'm a little late, but I'm glad to see you started without me." He nodded at Millie's drink. Rubbing his hands together, he continued. "So — I've been looking forward to this. Rosie's told me a lot about being at Woodley with all of you. In fact, walking over here, I thought up a little challenge for myself. I'm going to try to guess who's who based on what I can remember she's said." He looked at each one in turn. "Are you ready?"

"I don't know," Josie offered. "Depends on what she's told you about us."

"Ha! Nothing bad, I assure you. Actually, there are only a few general physical descriptions I can recall, so we'll see how well I do. Let me start with you." He squinted at Josie. "I think you are . . . Josie. You were quick to make a retort, you have intelligent brown eyes, and a calm demeanor. Am I right?"

Josie blushed. "Your identification is right. I don't know about the rest — but thanks."

"No problem. Now — I'm looking at the lady on my left. Let's see. You're petite, pixyish, you wear your dark hair very short, and you look inquisitive. I'm guessing you must be Millie."

Millie smiled and extended her hand. "You're right . . . and I'm guessing you're Mitch." Everyone laughed.

Mitch lowered his head and chuckled. "Uh, you're right — I didn't introduce myself. Good call. But, back to the game. The lady on my right has a fair complexion with a few freckles, fine hair, and a wide smile. You're Dottie, right?"

"Right, but you had a 50-50 chance. And now you can't go wrong guessing the last one, so *my guess* is that the game is over."

Mitch chuckled. "No, I'll add to the challenge by being more specific. I would have known anyway that Alex is next to Millie because she has gray-blue eyes and wavy hair that tends to frizz up when she's outside for long. Also, she's wearing an embroidered sweater that looks like it was made in Austria or Switzerland that she could have bought on one of her guided tours. He grinned at her. "How did I do?"

"You could have left out the 'frizzy hair' bit, but otherwise, you did well. Now, why don't you tell us about yourself. We haven't talked much about our husbands. We've just been trying to catch up with what we've been doing."

Mitch pulled on his chin. "Not much to tell. I've been the District Attorney of Mobile County for the past five years after working as an Assistant D.A. for eight. I oversee sixty employees and we have an excellent record of being tough on crime. Oh, and I met Rosie three years back when I worked on a community outreach program in the schools. She was heading up the anti-bullying program."

He glanced around. "But right now, I need a drink. Is that our waitress?" He pointed at the server at a nearby table.

"No," Rosemary said, "but I see her behind you heading this way. I'll wave her over."

Mitch twisted his neck to look, then quickly turned back and stared down at the table.

As Shirley walked up, her eyes widened. "Oh, so it's *you* that all the ladies were waiting for." Her laugh was husky. "Makes sense. What can I get for you, sweetie?"

"A vodka tonic. Thanks," Mitch mumbled without looking up.

After Shirley left, Rosemary frowned at him. "She acted like she knew you. I thought you never came here."

He shrugged indifferently. "She might have been involved in a case we prosecuted and remembers me as the D.A. Who knows? Apparently, I didn't send her to prison, so I can't say how she knows me. Anyway, let's talk about our Mardi Gras plans. I picked up my Braveheart costume today for the ball. I could be mistaken for Mel Gibson, except I'm not painting my face blue; but I've got the same plaid kilt, and sword, and shield. I've even got one of those fur purses they wear. I think they call it a sporran. And I'll wear a mask, of course. What are you going as, Rosie?"

"Mary, Queen of Scots — remember? I'll have to try to look like Sa-oir-se Ronan who played her in a movie, except I can't even pronounce her name. Anyway, I have a long dress with big sleeves and I made a big stand-up pleated collar for it. And then I have a crown, a mask, and a scepter. That's it."

"Y'all won't recognize her tomorrow night," Mitch said. "Or me. It's amazing how unrecognizable you are in a mask. I never know who the hell I'm talking to at one of these balls. It's great, though. There's a freedom in going incognito. You can do and say anything you want and get away with it."

Under her breath, Rosemary said, "You do, anyway," as Shirley brought Mitch his drink and set it down in front of him.

Just as he took a gulp, a balding man in a suit and tie came up behind him and clamped hands on his shoulders. "Counselor, you old devil. Five women in one night? Now you're getting greedy."

Mitch looked up, scowling. "Jenkins, for Christ's sake; that's my wife down at the end, and these are her friends."

The Public Defender lifted his palms and straightened. "Sorry, ladies. I was just teasing my old opponent, here — and maybe celebrating Mardi Gras a bit too much. We all tend to speak more freely when we're partying like this. My apologies." He nodded to Mitch. "See you around, counselor."

Rosemary glared at her husband.

"Don't even start, Rosie. The man's a drunk. I should have him removed from the P.D.'s office. Anyway, let's get out of here and go get some dinner. I'll take care of the check on our way out."

Rosemary remained seated with her arms folded, staring at Mitch as he fumbled with his wallet. The other women silently got up and headed for the door.

Chapter 11

THE NEXT MORNING the dining room at the Inn was abuzz over the preparations for the Mystic Goddesses' party which would be held in the courtyard that night.

Dottie carried her breakfast and coffee over to hold an empty table. She was soon joined by Millie who sat on the edge of her chair and drummed her fingers, waiting for the other two women to join them. After they arrived and sat down, Millie said, "Wait till I tell you guys what happened in our room last night."

"What?" the two asked in unison.

Millie drew in a deep breath and exhaled. "Well, when Dottie and I came back to the room last night after dinner and the parade, I went to turn on the lamp by my bed . . . but it wouldn't turn on. It had been on the night before so I took out the bulb to check it and see that the filament was intact. Then I looked under the bed at the outlet, and guess what? The lamp cord had been pulled out."

Dottie rolled her eyes. "So . . . Millie thinks there's a ghost in our room."

Millie nodded. "Of course, there's a ghost. Alex, you told us that dozens of people have reported lamps being unplugged here by ghosts."

"Live people can unplug lamps, too," Alex said, holding back her smile.

"I can assure you that neither of us crawled under the bed to unplug the lamp, right, Dottie?"

"No, I didn't, but —"

Josie jerked upright in her chair. "Wait a minute. *We* might have a ghost, too. I was the first one up today and the bathroom light was already on."

"I think it's more likely that I left it on last night," Alex suggested. "But I have to say I thought it was odd when we got home last night and saw that one of the wing chairs was turned away from the window. I suppose the cleaning people turned it, but why?"

Millie slid back in her chair. "It's ghosts—not cleaning people. Why else would there be so many reports about things moving around and lamps being unplugged if they had found some reasonable explanations. And don't forget the Lady in White who was murdered during Mardi Gras and now still waits for her date to the ball."

Alex shrugged. "I don't know. But how about the woman who swore that some spirit got in bed with her? Of course, she may have been drinking more spirits than seeing them. Anyway, speaking of ghoulish happenings, who wants to go with me down to the tunnel under the hotel? I'm going to ask Betsy at the front desk if someone can take me down this morning."

Dottie slowly lifted a hand. "If one of the custodians takes us, it should be okay. I don't want you to go alone."

"Okay, good." Alex turned to the others. "You two want to go on the ghost tour?. You might make some new friends."

Millie stuck out her tongue. "Funny. Speaking of new friends, what did you guys think of Mitch last night? I thought he could be quite charming, but I wouldn't trust him."

Alex tore off a piece of her beignet and chewed it. "Yeah, I agree. Rosemary's right that he has an 'answer for everything', although he seemed too defensive — like when the Public Defender teased him about being with several women."

Dottie twisted her mouth in thought. "That's true, but he was nice to us. I liked how he made up that little game to guess who we were. That showed he had an interest in Rosemary's friends — and in Rosemary, of course."

Josie nodded. "Good point. I think he was more relaxed at the seafood restaurant. Maybe he had been a little nervous on first meeting so many of us. Anyway, I don't think we can reach any conclusions about his character having spent just three hours with the guy."

"True," Alex agreed. "Rosemary still seemed upset with him after dinner when we watched the parade for a few minutes. Of course, that could have reminded her of seeing him with the redhead. Who knows? I think we should finish up here and go talk to Betsy about taking tours this morning."

As they walked into the lobby, Betsy was typing on her computer. Becoming aware of their presence, she looked up and smiled. "Oh, hi, ladies. What can I do for y'all?"

Alex spread her hands on the counter. "Well, Dottie and I were hoping Maria, or someone, could take us down to the tunnel. You had suggested that when I checked in a couple days ago. And Josie and Millie here would like to see the rooms in the Inn where there have been ghost sightings."

Betsy jutted out her lower lip. "Hmm. I'll call Maria and see about going down to the tunnel, but maybe come back in a half hour or so for me to conduct the ghost tour. I have some others asking about that. We've been busier 'than moths in mittens' today with that shindig tonight. Let me see about Maria."

Betsy punched numbers into a pager and the housekeeper soon appeared.

"Ah, here's Maria. Dear, would you have time to show these ladies the tunnel?"

Maria glanced over at the two women. "Lupe didn't come in today so I'm helping more with cleaning rooms, but I guess I could take them now for a few minutes."

"Yes, that would be wonderful. Thank you. Ladies, just follow Maria if you're ready. And, you other two ladies could maybe come back at ten?"

Betsy's attention became drawn to the front door as a delivery man entered pushing a hand truck piled high with cartons.

"Oh, dear, here comes the food from the caterer. I've gotta take care of this. I'll see y'all later. Good luck in the tunnel."

Maria nodded for Alex and Dottie to follow her as she led them out of the lobby and into the west townhouse then down the hallway toward the front.

As they approached the hidden panel, they heard footsteps coming down the stairs from the second floor. Presently, a man wearing a tool belt appeared around the corner.

Maria brightened. "Ah, Diego. *Buenos dias, mi amigo. Puedes mostrarles a estas damas el túnel?"*

Diego looked over at Alex and Dottie and nodded. "*Cierto.*"

Maria turned to speak to Alex. "Diego said he could take you. He can help you down there, okay?"

"Okay, sure. That's fine, Maria. You go back to your work."

"We'll need help?" Dottie said under her breath.

Alex held up her palms. "*Yo no se.*"

Diego pushed open the panel. Inside, his flashlight illuminated the closet-like space. As Alex and Dottie stood back, he leaned over and pulled up the small sheet of plywood that covered the two-foot square opening in the floor. He looked over at the women. "I'll go down first; then you, okay?"

Alex nodded. "Okay."

"This is crazy . . . or *loco*," Dottie said in a low voice.

Diego grunted as he squeezed through the hole and disappeared down the shaft, landing with a soft thud. Shining the flashlight up, he called out, "You come now."

Alex looked over at Dottie, raising her eyebrows to ask who should go first.

"You go," Dottie said. "I can wait."

Alex took a breath and gingerly stepped into the hole, holding onto the closet floor as she lowered herself, scraping against the rough sides of the opening. Exploring the space with one foot, she found purchase on one step and then another and another until she felt solid ground under her feet. "It's fine, Dottie. Come on down."

Dottie made grumbling noises while she squirmed through the opening, slid down and landed on the tunnel floor. Squatting, she looked up at Alex who was illuminated by the flashlight. "What's fine about it? We can't even stand up."

Alex turned to Diego. "Is the whole tunnel as low as this?"

"No, we can stand in some of it. Follow me."

The two women inched along behind him until he stopped to shine his light into an alcove. "There's an old bed," he said, pointing to the dilapidated frame of what had once been an army cot.

Alex giggled. "What's left of it. The canvas is totally eaten away. Hard to believe someone ever stayed overnight down here."

Diego nodded. "They say ghosts of soldiers are still here."

"This looks like a place a ghost would like," Dottie said. "Maybe, let's go a little further and then head back? All right with you, Alex?"

"Sure. I just want to see where it opens up."

Twenty minutes later they came to the entrance of a higher chamber. Diego shone the light around the space which revealed three stone archways about thirty feet across from them. "Those arches lead to another tunnel. See, you can almost stand up in here."

Illustrating, he straightened his legs, but kept his head down to clear the ceiling.

Dottie hunched her shoulders and walked in a small circle, swinging her arms from her shoulders like an ape. "Oh, this is much better."

Alex laughed. "Okay, I guess we've seen enough, Diego. We can go back now."

"Okay." He turned and squatted down to reenter the previous tunnel, then continued moving crablike in a crouched position.

"Oof!" Dottie cried out as she stumbled over a board. "I'm not sure even ghosts want to stay here."

Alex patted her on the back. "Somehow I don't think you're enjoying this. Don't worry, we won't come down here again."

Twenty minutes later Diego wrested himself up out of the hole and extended a hand to help Alex and then Dottie.

Alex brushed the dust and cobwebs off her clothes and shook out her hair. "That's better. *Gracias,* Diego. I for one enjoyed that."

"I for two didn't," Dottie said, then grinned. "No, it was interesting to see how it was when Confederate soldiers were there; except they didn't have flashlights."

Alex's eyes widened. "You're right. We probably should have carried candles. Anyway, let's go upstairs and clean up and see if Josie and Millie are around. I'd like to explore the historic district for a while before we need to dress for the party."

"I would, too. Maybe get back in time to rest up a little for the ball. I've never been to a celebration as big as they're saying this will be. I can't wait."

Chapter 12

ALEX GINGERLY STEPPED into the navy satin dress and wriggled her arms into the long sleeves. Holding the back together with one hand, she gathered the full long skirt with the other and hobbled over to the dresser. "Could you help me here, Josie? This dress needs a second person to get into it."

Josie walked up behind her and pulled up the long zipper in back. "There . . . got it. Nice dress — almost as nice as your bridesmaid's dress."

Alex chuckled as she pressed down on the deep pleat in the front of the skirt. Checking herself in the mirror, she looked approvingly at her auburn hair that was now softly waved and under control, even though she knew it would frizz up after being out in the night air for a while. "I got this dress for formal nights on cruises—which are almost a thing of the past now. It's kinda fun to wear, though."

Josie looked down at her emerald green velvet skirt and beaded sweater. "I got this for someone's wedding a few years back. I'd say it makes up in comfort for what it lacks in fun."

"It looks great. The right color for Mardi Gras, too. I see your skirt has pockets. Would you mind keeping the room key so I don't need to take my purse?"

Josie nodded. "Sure. Anything else?"

"No. I'll carry my ticket that we'll hand in. If I need something else, I'll ask you for the key."

Hearing a knock, both women turned to look, then walked over to the door. Alex peered through the peephole and jerked back.

"Hey, it's me—Rosemary," the familiar voice was heard saying from the hallway.

Alex swung the door open to admit their visitor who strode in wearing a long purple gown and holding up a scepter. Turning slowly, she showed off her costume with its skirt held out by crinolines, its puffy sleeves, and the pleated stand-up collar that came up to her ears. Completing the outfit was an embroidered sleeveless surcoat. Coming back around, only her smile was recognizable as her face was all but covered with a glittery mask that sprouted yellow, blue, and green feathers out of the top and sides. On her head sat a six-pointed gold crown set with paste jewels.

Alex stood back, wide-eyed. "Is that really you, Rosemary?"

Their guest pushed up the mask to reveal her eyes. "Who else would come to your room dressed as Mary Queen of Scots?"

Josie was running her fingers over the brocade fabric. "This is amazing. You really could pass for a Medieval queen — except for the mask."

"Yeah, that and the fact that the Middle Ages ended five hundred years ago."

"There is that," Alex agreed. "Josie and I were just saying that we thought we were pretty dressed up. Compared to you, we look like we're going to a Longhorn Steak House for dinner."

Rosemary snickered. "I think you look great. You can't help it that you're not Goddesses."

Alex gave her a look. "Right. So, would you like to sit down, Goddess? Or does your head have to always be higher than ours?"

Rosemary stuck out her tongue. "I just came to get you to go to the party. I changed into this costume in Millie's and Dottie's room. They were just finishing dressing when I left. When I came up, people were already streaming into the hotel."

"What about Mitch? Didn't you come with him?" Alex asked.

"Yeah, he's down there. He wanted to see what was going on and get a drink and whatever. I told him I'd be staying with you guys most of the night. He and I are barely speaking right now, anyway."

Alex sighed. "Sorry to hear that. Do you want to tell us about it?"

"There's nothing to tell, really. I'm just fed up. The man has been making a fool out of me and I've kept hoping he would change. After three years, I realize he's not going to. Listening to that Public

Defender's remark last night, I looked at the contacts Mitch has on his cell phone. There were several women's names I didn't recognize — right there, out in the open. The guy is unbelievable."

Alex shook her head. "That's really too bad. I don't understand it, but there it is. Sounds like you need to take some action at this point—maybe a trial separation."

"Better than a trial for murder," Rosemary said sourly. "No, I need to get a lawyer and see how I can be protected from Mitch. Since he's the top prosecutor in the county, that might discourage a lot of attorneys from going against him."

Josie patted her friend's shoulder. "You're getting ahead of yourself. You don't know if that's the case or not. I think tonight, you need to put all that out of your mind and enjoy the party."

Rosemary's mouth twitched from side to side, considering. "You're right. This will be a great party and I'm lucky to have all of you here with me. Anyway, I'm a lot better off than the real Mary Stuart. She spent the last twenty years of her life in prison and then was beheaded."

"Oh, that's a fun fact," Josie said. "I think it's time we left for the party. Is everyone ready?"

Alex glanced over at the dresser. "I said I'd leave my purse here so I'll just grab my ID and a lipstick to put in your pocket, Josie. How about you, Rosemary?"

She patted a pouch on her weskit. "I put a few things in here so I don't have to walk around with a purse, either. You guys have your room key, right? You can always come back up here if you need something else. If you're ready, let's go see about Dottie and Millie. I could use a glass of wine and something to eat and I'm sure you could, too."

Chapter 13

WHEN THEY STEPPED OUTSIDE, they were transfixed by the sight and sounds of the courtyard. The space had been transformed into a kaleidoscope of swirling colors, lights, and music, while a crowd of revelers stood talking and laughing.

Overhead, strings of multi-colored lights had been strung to festoon the square, floating in the blackness, crisscrossing back and forth between the hotel's wings, the rear building, and the original hotel.

On ground level, golden lights peeked out from behind shrubbery, from inside flower pots, along curved pathways, and around the fountain, illuminating the low curved wall and the burbling water that splashed down from the top, cascading down to the basin from tier to tier.

Wrought iron café tables, set up around the perimeter, were softly lit by flickering candles of all sizes: tapers, pillars, and votives were set around everywhere.

The party appeared to be in full swing as formally-garbed guests mixed in with costumed Mystic Goddesses and their spouses whose disguises included face-covering masks and gaudy outfits replete with feathers and sequins on purple, gold, and green fabrics. They were a hodgepodge of characters. Ballerinas twirled around peacocks who fanned out their tails for jokers and clowns, while kings and queens strolled by in regal splendor.

On a platform erected at one end of the square, singers and a band performed a variety of musical forms including soulful blues, jazz riffs, and contemporary rock. As they got into the Carnival atmosphere, the trumpets wailed, the reeds vibrated, and the drums kept up an insistent beat of up-tempo rhythms.

The crowd flowed from the Inn's lobby out into the courtyard and around back to the Carriage House. It was a lively mixture of talking, dancing, eating, and drinking. No one just sat quietly.

Buffet tables inside and outside groaned under the weight of mounded serving dishes heaped with colorful appetizers like decorative canapes, stuffed mushrooms, crab puffs, gourmet cheeses and crackers, as well as dessert offerings of chocolate mousse, cream puffs, fruit tarts, and spiced walnuts.

The hotel staff circulated among the guests replenishing plates of food and serving drinks to supplement the bar service in the Carriage House and the temporary bar that had been set up in the courtyard.

After the women had stood looking around for several minutes, Millie shouted to them, "Shouldn't we get some food and something to drink and find a place to sit?"

"We can try," Rosemary answered. "Let's go into the lobby where it might be a little quieter, at least."

As they made it through the crowd up to the door into the hotel, they had to stand back and wait as people came and went in a steady stream. When there was a momentary break, Millie grabbed the handle and held the door open, telling Rosemary to go through first as she had to hold onto her scepter and her wide gown. Once they were all inside, Rosemary pointed her scepter to a vacant corner. "Let's go over there."

Slowly making their way around groups of people who stood talking, they gathered near the corner, out of the flow of traffic.

Rosemary exhaled and straightened her crown. "Whew! Okay—I think we need teamwork here. How about if two of us get into the buffet line to pick up food for everyone, and the rest of us get drinks. Is white wine okay with everyone to make it simple?"

They all nodded.

"We could try to find a place to sit in that lounge where you and I were Sunday," Alex suggested.

"Dottie and I can get the food and take it there," Millie volunteered.

Dottie's shoulders dropped. "Oh, thanks. That's like sending us into battle with this crowd."

"Just follow me. I can find an opening to slip into without anyone noticing."

Alex gave a little snort. "You have to watch her, Dottie. When we were in Europe on the school tour, she and I got stuck in a crowd in Munich. She told me to start yelling 'Platz!' to get past people; that it was considered polite."

Millie snickered. "Oh, yeah. I can't believe you remember that. Anyway, you caught on so it wasn't any fun."

Dottie gave her an eye roll. "We'll wait our turn. Besides, there are people here who are carrying swords."

Rosemary tapped her scepter on the wall to get their attention. "Okay. Let's get going. We'll meet again in a few minutes in the lounge down the hall past the reception desk."

"I think you're having way too much fun being queen," Josie cracked as they started to make their way back into the crowd.

"Should the three of us go to the bar in the Carriage House?" Alex asked, "Or, maybe first look for one of the hotel staff carrying trays of drinks. I think I saw Diego, one of the porters, wearing an apron. They may be circulating with red and white wine."

The three of them made it to the back door and out into the courtyard with little trouble. As they stopped to look around, Josie pointed off to their left. "There's an outdoor bar over there that doesn't look too busy."

"Oh, and that's Diego who's one of the bartenders," Alex said.

A few minutes later they were following the porter back into the Inn as he carried a bottle of wine and five glasses on a tray.

With Diego leading the way, they continued through the lobby and down the hall to the lounge that was then occupied by only two other guests seated by a window.

As Diego paused in the doorway, Alex slipped past him into the room. "We'll be sitting in these loveseats if you'd like to put your tray down on the coffee table. Dottie and our other friend should be here momentarily."

Just then Millie appeared in the doorway with Dottie behind her.

"Oh, they're here now," Alex added.

The two women came in and set plates down next to the tray. Diego twisted off the cap on the bottle and filled the glasses. "Can I get you ladies anything else right now?"

"No," Alex answered, "but thanks for helping us out."

Diego made a small bow, picked up the tray and left the room.

Dottie passed around paper plates. "We took some of everything so there should be things you like. Help yourself."

Rosemary sat in the frame chair pulled up between the loveseats, removed her mask and arranged her skirt around her. "Ah, that's better. It's not easy walking around in a hoop skirt and looking through feathers. This is nice. I'm glad we can sit here and enjoy our food for a few minutes before we have to go back out there and join the party. It would be nice to dance, though. I'm sure Mitch would indulge me."

Josie took a bite of a crab cake. "I'm looking forward to seeing see him in his Braveheart costume."

Rosemary snuffled. "He won't be hard to spot. I'm sure he's the only man out there in a kilt. He's probably the only one I'll be able to recognize. That reminds me — I read recently that masks were first worn in the Middle Ages so you'd be unrecognizable to escape death. They figured that if the devil doesn't know it's you, he won't take you."

"Hah! That makes sense," Millie said. "Of course, that means all of us guests are susceptible to die." She held up her hands and wriggled her fingers to play-act like a departed sprit. "O-o-o-h."

"Did you have one of these cream puffs?" Josie asked. "I'm changing the subject to something more pleasant. They're delicious. By the way, Rosemary, I haven't seen anyone taking tickets."

"I think that's because we came down from upstairs. They have a hand stamp to try to keep track of people who pay, but there are so many entrances here I'm sure they miss a lot of people and plenty of people come in off the street, too. Between having a lot of doors and half the people being in disguise, it's hard to control who should be here and who shouldn't."

A half hour later they were all back outside, joining the crowd celebrating the last few hours of Mardi Gras. As the five-some inched their way around the courtyard, many people they passed complimented Rosemary on her outfit and inquired about who she was supposed to be. Rosemary identified herself as Mary Stuart, but didn't reveal her own identity.

"Why don't you tell them who you are?" Millie asked.

"Because—that's the fun of it. Everyone's anonymous, unless you happen to know their costume. Speaking of which, I see Mitch over there. Let's go see what he's been up to."

They approached him as he was standing next to the fountain chatting with a tall man dressed in a tuxedo. When Rosemary walked up, Mitch did a double-take.

Rosemary hesitated a moment before speaking. "Hi. I didn't mean to interrupt. I just wanted to see how you're doing."

Mitch cleared his throat. "Dennis, this is my wife, Rosemary — I think. I hadn't seen her as Mary Stuart up until now." He angled his head toward the other man. "This is Denny Rivers. Denny's an attorney in private practice. Friend of the Halversteins."

Rosemary nodded and smiled politely. "Ah. Good people. Nice to meet you, Ken." Turning back to Mitch, she said, "The girls wanted to see you in your costume."

Rivers held up a hand and took a step back. "Y'all go on and visit. We were just talking shop."

Mitch nodded to him, then flashed a smile at the four women. "So, whaddya think? Can you see me invading northern England?"

Millie tilted her head as she scrutinized his black mask, beret, and long-haired wig, then moved down to his Jacobite shirt, studded doublet, fake fur sporran bag, plaid kilt, and knee socks with heavy leather shoes. "Yes, but it's probably not a good idea. I won't even ask what you're wearing underneath your kilt."

Mitch laughed. "And I won't tell you. I'll just say I'm glad it's not too chilly tonight." He laughed again. "Well, enough of that. Have you guys eaten? I've just had a couple crab cakes."

"We ate in a lounge in the hotel," Rosemary answered. "If you want to get some food and something to drink, I'll hold a table and sit with you. There are a couple empty ones out here. We found a quiet spot inside . . . even had our own bartender carry our wine in for us. Alex knew him from when he took her down to the tunnel. He was tending the bar that's set up on the other side of the fountain."

Mitch raised his eyebrows, considering. "Well, if you're sure you want to . . . I'd like to have you keep me company."

Dottie put a hand on Rosemary. "Go ahead. Don't worry about us. We'll walk around some more; maybe get out on the dance floor."

"Good idea," Alex said. "I see they're starting a line dance if anyone's up for that. We'll check back with you in a while. I'm sure we won't have trouble finding you wherever you are."

The four women made their way over to the section of the courtyard that had been set aside for dancing and joined the back row of line dancers. They tried to mimic the moves of the dancers in the row in front of them, but were usually one step behind and facing the wrong way most of the time.

"I don't get how everyone else knows which way to turn!" Millie complained.

"I think they do this more than once a year," Alex answered.

After the line dance, they sat out for a couple minutes to catch their breath before going back in to try a calypso number.

"I'd like to find a ladies' room," Josie announced the next time they took a break. "In fact, why don't we go up to the room?"

"Let's do that," Alex agreed.

When they came downstairs a half hour later, people were surging around the fountain dancing and singing along with the band that was playing *When the Saints Go Marching In*.

"I don't think we can find Mitch and Rosemary in this crowd," Josie said. "How about we make our way over to the Carriage House? I could use another glass of wine or a cup of coffee or something."

"Good idea," Dottie agreed. "Rosemary may be over there. If not, we can come back and look for her after this crowd breaks up a little."

The bar at the carriage house was crowded and noisy with people trying to talk over each other and to drown out the rock music coming from the band playing in the next room.

"What do you think?" Alex asked after they had pushed their way just inside the door and stood flattened against a wall.

"I think I'd like to be in the lounge in the Inn," Millie responded. "Good thing Rosemary isn't with us. She could never fit in here with that big dress of hers."

Alex checked her watch. "I think it's been almost an hour since we left her. Let's go back out and try to find her again. If we do, maybe we can all go back inside the hotel."

Several minutes later they were back outside, slowly moving through the crowd, turning their heads left and right to look for Mitch or Rosemary.

As they made their way to the other side of the fountain, they caught a glimpse of a purple dress within a circle of women dressed as flappers and chorus girls.

"Rosemary!" Millie called out.

Moments later, Rosemary emerged, waving at them. "Hi, you guys! I was just talking with some women in the Goddesses. I hope you haven't had a hard time finding me."

"Oh, no," Dottie answered. "How could you think that?" she asked, grinning.

Rosemary shook her scepter at her. "It was your idea for me to stay with Mitch while he got some dinner. Which I did. Then he saw some friends, so I left him a little while ago."

"We were thinking we'd see if we could get another glass of wine, and go inside for a while; see if that lounge is still nearly empty," Alex said.

Just then, the band stopped playing in the middle of a phrase and a woman's voice was heard speaking over the public address system, "Is there a doctor in the house? We have an emergency! Is there a doctor here?!"

One man in formal dress raised his hand and hurried toward the platform as the crowd parted to let him through.

"This way!" the woman called out, stepping off the stage and waving the man on as she took off across the courtyard.

"That's Betsy," Alex said. "They're coming our way."

The women watched as the two people ran past them.

"Let's go see what's happening," Alex said, gesturing for the others to follow.

As they made their way through the crowd to the other side of the fountain, they spotted the doctor kneeling at the edge of the courtyard tending to someone on the ground. Betsy stood by nervously shifting her weight from one foot to the other, her hands clasped together. After a couple minutes, the doctor looked up at her and slowly shook his head. Betsy cried out, then clamped a hand over her mouth. As the doctor got to his feet, he stepped away from the figure on the pavement, revealing red plaid fabric worn by the person who lay there, motionless.

Chapter 14

ROSEMARY GASPED and clutched at her throat. "That's Mitch's kilt!"

Wincing, Alex turned to the others. "You all stay here with Rosemary while I go see what happened."

Rosemary shook her head. "No, I'm going with you!"

"Okay," Alex answered, "but just the two of us."

Impatiently, they looked for an opening in the crowd that had started to gather and was blocking their view of the person on the ground.

Betsy had positioned herself between the onlookers and the doctor with her arms outstretched like an umpire calling a player 'safe' in baseball. "Stand back! Everyone, please stand back! We've got a medical emergency here! An ambulance will be here momentarily and they need room to get through."

People slowly started backing up. "*Thank* you, thank you," Betsy said.

Alex and Rosemary finally managed to get to the front through the retreating crowd. Alex, out of breath, caught hold of the manager. "Betsy, my friend and I need to see the doctor. I think that's her husband who's sick."

"Who's your friend?"

"Rosemary Stuart. She's right here. She's the one who came to visit me when I arrived, remember? Anyway, her husband is wearing a red plaid kilt. We could see that same fabric on whoever is on the ground behind the doctor."

Betsy's shoulders slumped as she looked past Alex to focus on the woman behind her. "Are you Rosemary Stuart?"

"Yes, and I think that's my husband, Mitch Stuart, who the doctor's treating. What's wrong with him? I need to get over there."

Betsy let out a sigh. "I'm sorry, Mrs. Stuart. Yes . . . I'm afraid that it is your husband. We found his identification in his purse. The doctor tried to help him but I'm sorry to say that he . . . that he didn't make it."

"What? What do you mean he *'didn't make it'*? Are you telling me he's dead? That's impossible. He was perfectly healthy a half hour ago."

Betsy bit down on her lower lip. "All I can tell you is that two people came into the lobby to tell me a man out here was having some kind of seizure. I ran out to see and immediately called for an ambulance. Then, as you know, I went on stage to ask for help and Dr. Kendall responded but it was too late. I'm so sorry." She took hold of Rosemary's arm. "Here, come and talk to the doctor. I shouldn't be trying to explain what happened."

Betsy guided a shaking Rosemary over to where Dr. Kendall stood protectively in front of the body. Alex followed at a distance and stayed back, out of the way.

Rosemary tried to twist away from Betsy to get a better look. As she broke free, she lunged forward, which alarmed the doctor who grabbed her, pinning her arms against her chest. "Excuse me, but *who* are you?"

"I'm Rosemary Stuart, and that's my husband! I just want to know what happened to him. The manager told me he's dead, but he can't be. He was perfectly fine all evening. I ate dinner with him not an hour ago."

The doctor relaxed his grip. "Okay, okay, calm down. First, would you please remove your mask."

Rosemary ripped it off and stuffed it in the pocket of her weskit. "Sorry, but I need to know—"

The doctor held up a hand. "I'll tell you what I know, Ms. Stuart. Let me first introduce myself — I'm Dr. Evan Kendall. I'm an internist here in Mobile. Your husband suffered a fatal catastrophic event that I haven't yet been able to diagnose. Tell me, has he been treated for any heart problems?"

"No. No. He's never even been to a cardiologist, to my knowledge."

"Did he have any food allergies?"

"Food allergies? None that I know of. Anyway, I'm sure he didn't eat anything here that he hasn't had many times before, so that doesn't make sense. Are you suggesting he died from something he ate tonight?"

Kendall raised one shoulder. "I don't know. I know he had a sudden and violent reaction to *something*. Did he happen to eat any almonds tonight?"

Rosemary screwed up her face. "Almonds? I didn't see any. I know he ate a few of the spiced walnuts, but he's had those before. He doesn't have a peanut allergy, either. This is crazy. Can I just see him?"

Kendall shook his head. "I'm sorry, but not yet. "Like I say, we need to first determine the cause of death, whether or not it's from natural causes. At this point, only an autopsy would be conclusive."

Rosemary's eyes widened in alarm. "An autopsy? I don't want an autopsy."

"I understand your feelings, Ms. Stuart, but—"

"No, I don't think you do. I should have a say in whether my husband is to be filleted like a trout."

Kendall drew a hand across his brow. "Ms. Stuart, in the state of Alabama, the District Attorney — or even any circuit judge — can order an autopsy in a suspicious death or any death due to unnatural causes."

Rosemary scoffed, "Mitch *was* the District Attorney. And there can't be anything suspicious or unnatural about his death. He must have had an aneurism or something that couldn't have been foreseen."

Kendall looked past her toward the Inn. "I see the EMTs are coming now with the police. The ambulance will be taking your husband's body to Providence Memorial, where I happen to be on staff. I'll need to first sign the Pronouncement of Death and then the police will have to assess the scene."

Rosemary turned and looked helplessly at Alex, then back to the doctor. "'Assess the scene'? I just can't believe this is happening."

Kendall raised his hands with his palms facing her. "Please, we need to know what we're dealing with here. It's possible that someone at the party did something to cause your husband's attack. The police will be conducting an initial investigation to determine what other personnel may be needed. Right now, I have to ask you and your friend to sit over there to and wait while the police go over the area."

As the women headed where Kendall had pointed, he walked out to meet the EMTs and two uniformed policemen, gesturing for them to get in a huddle to discuss the situation. After several minutes, he turned and pointed in the direction of the body, then towards Rosemary who had her head down, dabbing her eyes with a tissue.

As the circle broke up, Kendall led the police in the direction of the body while the two technicians stayed behind with the gurney.

Arriving at the scene, Kendall remained with Betsy while the two cops scoped out the area before approaching the deceased. Bending over, they looked closely at the body, being careful not to touch it or to disturb the area. After conferring with each other, they walked away. One of them used his two-way radio while the other removed a spool of yellow tape out of a leather case and started unrolling it in a circle, keeping the perimeter about ten feet away from the body, to include a nearby table and two chairs. Imprinted on the tape were the words, "Do No Cross. Police Line."

Having completed that task, the two officers waved Kendall over. After a few minutes of conversation with the cops, he headed over to speak to Rosemary.

"Okay, Ms. Stuart," he began, squatting in front of her. "The officers have completed their preliminary inspection, and they agree with me that the death is suspicious, so they're treating this as a crime scene at this point."

Rosemary's reddened eyes flew open.

"Now, that may change, but that's where things stand now. The Medical Examiner has been called, along with a CSI team and a detective."

Rosemary slumped in her chair. "I - I just can't believe that someone here could have done anything on purpose to bring on some kind of seizure. In the first place, Mitch was wearing a disguise, so who would even know it was him? *I* wouldn't have known him if I hadn't seen his costume before he got dressed. His face was mostly covered by his mask, and he had on a wig and a kilt and all."

Kendall shrugged and shook his head. "He may have revealed his identity to some people here, or he may have told others about his costume in advance of the party."

Rosemary glanced sideways at Alex. "As far as I know, we only discussed the party and our costumes with a few close friends."

Kendall looked off into the distance with his chin raised. "Here comes the M.E. and a forensic team now. After they're finished with their examination, and recorded and released the scene, you'll be allowed to say goodbye to your husband."

As the doctor walked off, Rosemary leaned against Alex, dissolving in tears.

Alex put her arm around her. "I know. I know. This is a nightmare, but you're doing fine. We'll all help you get through this. And don't worry that the police are involved. That's normal procedure when there's a sudden, unexplained death like this."

"'*Suspicious death,*' according to the doctor," Rosemary said shakily, dabbing at her cheeks with a fresh tissue she had pulled out of her pocket. "Oh, now who are these people coming?"

Chapter 15

ALEX AND ROSEMARY watched stone-faced as two men and a young woman, all in white lab coats and carrying satchels, strode past them headed to the newly designated 'crime scene.' The woman also had a 35 mm camera hanging around her neck.

When they arrived at the secured area, they carefully stepped over the yellow tape; the two men staying just inside, while the female technician walked around taking pictures of the general vicinity of the courtyard as well as the area inside the warning-tape circle.

Over at the body, she changed lenses and photographed the victim's head, torso and extremities from all angles. Then, kneeling down, she adjusted her lens for close-ups from head to feet. Sitting back on her haunches, she scrutinized the form for a couple of minutes, then took a few more shots of the face. Finished, she turned and nodded to the other team members who were waiting. Getting to her feet, she lifted the camera from around her neck and walked back to the tape line, speaking briefly to the M.E. and to her fellow forensic scientist.

The older, greying Medical Examiner pulled on a pair of latex gloves before he knelt by the body and clasped the victim's wrist, then placed a hand over the chest. Peering through his bifocals, he pushed up the eyelids and shone a penlight into the vacant eyes. He then examined the mouth, ears, and nose. Bending down, he sniffed around the victim's face. The doctor's forehead was furrowed with concern as he stood and walked slowly around the body.

Meanwhile, the male CSI was applying a fine powder over the table and the arms of the two chairs. After dusting them, he pressed small squares of clear tape onto where he saw fingerprints and transferred each one onto matching papers. He continued the procedure over the entire table top and on the four arms of the chairs.

Dusting the outside of the drinking glass, he repeated the process of picking up prints and transferring them to papers.

Then, reaching into his satchel, he pulled out a box of cotton swabs and was about to swirl one in the bottom of the glass. When he peered into it using a flashlight, he stared in disbelief at a layer of white powder remaining on the bottom. Slowly pushing the glass away, he called over his fellow CSI member and the Medical Examiner.

As they joined him at the table, the M.E. dipped one of the cotton swabs into the bottom of the glass, transferring specks of white crystals which he touched with the tip of his tongue, wincing at the taste. Turning to the CSI technicians, he spoke quietly, solemnly nodding. Taking another swab, he collected a fresh sample of the residue which he deposited into a plastic bag, sealed it, and laid it on the table.

The two CSI members labelled the bag and deposited it into a paper sack, then walked over to the body to continue their investigation. Using clean swabs, they collected saliva from the victim's mouth and mucous from his nose. They then went over the victim's clothing and collected any foreign fibers and hairs.

As they were finishing, they heard footsteps and looked up. They nodded to acknowledge the familiar man who was approaching. He was a man of about forty, dressed in an ordinary brown checked sport coat and khaki trousers. What distinguished him was his attitude of swagger, as well as the fierce intelligence seen in his dark hooded eyes.

"Detective Langford," the M.E. called out.

"Dr. Harris," responded the policeman to complete the shorthand exchange.

"Got anything?" Langford again.

"I'll be right with you, Drew."

That gave Langford a few moments to survey the crowd in the courtyard, contemplating the feasibility of questioning a veritable sea of suspects. If there had been a criminal wrongdoing that caused the death, no one here would have an alibi that could eliminate them. On the other hand, if one put aside having opportunity, there might be just a few people who had a clear motive: a death benefit, or a score to settle. The deceased was the county District Attorney. He undoubtedly had made enemies in the performance of his job. Maybe in his social life, too. Of course, Langford didn't yet know if the death would be ruled a homicide by the CSI and M.E. Maybe the poor shit had had a heart attack.

The band struck up the familiar Eagles' hit, "Take it Easy." Langford started singing along under his breath:

"Take it easy, take it easy

Don't let the sound of your own wheels drive you crazy.

Lighten up while you still can

Don't even try to understand

Just find a place to make your stand

And take it easy."

Looking over to the secured area, he lifted his chin in acknowledgement of the Medical Examiner who was heading his way. As the M.E. got closer, Langford noticed the man's grim expression. "George, are you finished at this end?"

"Yeah, I'm all done here. Now it's your turn."

Langford winced. "So, it is a homicide? You've determined cause?"

"I'd say a generous dose of potassium cyanide would do in most people."

Chapter 16

DETECTIVE LANGFORD took a breath. "Yowzah. You don't need a chemical analysis?"

Harris smiled smugly, "Not if you can recognize the taste of bitter almonds — and can find crystals in the bottom of a drinking glass that's on the table next to a corpse. Not to mention that there are witnesses who saw the deceased gasping for air and turning red before he keeled over."

Langford pressed his hair back with both hands. "Well, the good news is the perp is someone who's here at the hotel. The bad news is that includes about 250 people. But who knows; maybe, I'll get lucky with my early interviews."

Harris shrugged. "You could start with the hotel manager, Betsy Davis. She was called to the scene by a couple who must have seen Stuart right after he ingested the poison since it kills in about three minutes. Ms. Davis called the ambulance, then asked for a doctor here. This guy Kendall tried to give assistance, but it was too late. He had the responding officers call for CSI as he judged it a suspicious death. He's signed the Proclamation for time of death. I understand he talked to the wife and got some background intel."

Hearing that, Langford raised his eyebrows. "I should start with her. Statistically, there's an over 40 per cent chance that she's the perp."

Harris waved his hand dismissively. "You've been watching too much TV. Anyway, her name's Rosemary. She's the one in the purple and a crown on her head sitting over there staring at us."

Langford chuckled. "Yeah, I'll get to her. I want to see the body first—if CSI is done with processing the scene. Then you can transport the corpse to the morgue at Providence."

The M.E. glanced over at the crime scene. "They're almost finished, I think. Sharon might still be sketching; I dunno. I'll walk over and introduce you to Kendall and Ms. Davis standing by the tape. The doctor's the tall guy in a tux and the manager's the lady with the fancy hairdo next to him."

Walking over to the pair, the M.E. made the introductions and Langford continued on to the body, walking slowly around it before bending over to inspect the victim's face. Shaking his head, he turned and went back to join the others.

"Ms. Davis, do you know the guests who reported the deceased having a seizure?"

Betsy bit down on her lower lip and shook her head ruefully. "No. It was a man and a woman, but they were wearing masks and in costume. I didn't think to take their names. I've looked around for them, but I didn't want to leave the taped-off area; I wanted to keep anyone from crossing the line."

Langford nodded in understanding. "You were right to stay here, but I'll need you to locate them so I can talk to them. Did they seem to know Stuart? — use his name, or say they were with him — anything like that?"

Betsy's brow creased in thought. "No, I'm sure they said they 'saw a man having a fit' like they weren't *with* him and didn't know him."

Langford patted her shoulder. "Okay, that'll do for now, but I'd like you to use the microphone to summon them to the lobby. Just say you'd like to speak with the couple who came to report a man who was 'sick out in the courtyard'. Don't give out any more information about the incident. We're dealing with a murder here."

Betsy blanched and put her hand to her chest. "Oh, my stars! There hasn't been a murder in this hotel for fifty years — and the young lady who was killed then turned into a ghost who's haunted this place ever since."

Langford looked down at his shoes to hide his smile before he commented. "I'm sorry this has happened on your watch, Ms. Davis. At the same time, I know that legends like the 'Lady in White' don't hurt business in Mobile."

He turned to Dr. Kendall to ask for a summary of his interview with Rosemary Stuart and he responded with a concise but thorough recollection.

When he finished reciting the facts, Langford asked, "How would you characterize her reaction to her husband's death?"

Kendall stroked his chin. "Well, at first she was in denial. As I told you, she had been with him for at least part of the evening and he had seemed to be feeling fine, according to her."

"Did she seem upset by his death?"

"More shocked — at least initially. Then, yes, she cried. I'm sure she was upset."

"Did you tell her he had been murdered?"

"No, I didn't use that word. I did tell her that someone could have done something to bring on the fatal attack. That it was a suspicious death."

"Okay, that's fine. Thanks, doctor. You've been very helpful. I'll go speak with her now."

Langford ambled over to where Rosemary and Alex were sitting, aware of the women's penetrating stares as he approached. "Mrs. Stuart? Rosemary Stuart?"

Rosemary stiffened. "Yes, I'm Rosemary."

"Ms. Stuart, I'm Detective Drew Langford of the Mobile police department. I'm here to ask you a few questions."

Langford looked over at Alex. "Are you a friend of Ms. Stuart's?"

"Yes. I'm Alex Trotter — an old friend from college. I'm just visiting along with three others from our school. Dr. Kendall said I could sit with her while the police were investigating her husband's death."

"That's fine, but I need to talk to Ms. Stuart alone right now. I'll want to speak with you and the others a bit later so don't any of you leave the hotel and don't discuss the case."

Alex nodded and rose from her chair. Patting Rosemary's shoulder, she said, "I'll find the others and we'll see you later, okay?"

Rosemary eyes brimmed with tears. "O-o-kay. See you later."

Langford proceeded to sit in the chair Alex had vacated and set a small case on the ground next to him. Pulling a small notebook from it, he flipped it open, and poised a pen over it. Turning toward Rosemary, he smiled. "I know this is upsetting, Ms. Stuart, but try to relax. I have just a few things to ask you." His eyes travelled from her crown down her outfit to her shoes. "By the way, that's quite an elaborate costume you're wearing. Who are you supposed to be?"

Rosemary dabbed at her eyes and cleared her throat. "Well, I'm *supposed to be* Mary, Queen of Scots."

Langford's mouth twitched back and forth. "Ah, I get it. She was a Stuart, too, so you almost share the same name."

Rosemary brightened. "That's right. You must know your Scottish history."

Langford chuckled. "Not really. I saw the movie with what's-her-name Ronan. As I recall, Mary was sent to prison before being beheaded." He blinked at Rosemary. "But you're the younger Queen, of course. So, anyway, getting down to business, let me tell you I've already spoken to Dr. Kendall about your conversation with him, so I know that you were with your husband part of the evening and you felt that he was in good health."

Rosemary swallowed hard and looked down at the ground. "That's right. I sat with him while he ate his dinner so I know that he was feeling good and that he ate what I had eaten earlier, so I don't understand if it's the food that made him sick."

Langford studied her neat profile. "What did he have to drink?"

Rosemary turned to face him. "His usual, I think. A vodka tonic."

"Did you get it for him?"

Rosemary blinked. "No. He brought it back to the table — from the courtyard bar, I think. I didn't see him get it."

The detective raised an eyebrow. "You indicated that you had already eaten. Why didn't you have your dinner with him?"

Rosemary looked down again and shredded her tissue. "We had agreed that I would spend most of the evening with my friends. They're only in town for a few days. We all lived together for four years in college; first in a dorm and then in a house off-campus. Until this week we hadn't seen each other since we graduated ten years ago."

Langford wrote in his notebook, then looked up. "Where were you when your husband was having a seizure?"

Rosemary jerked around to look the detective in the eye. "I don't know exactly when that was, so I don't know where I was. I know I wasn't there when he had whatever kind of fit it was."

Langford covered his cough with his hand. "Okay, what time was it when you sat with him as he ate his dinner?"

"I wasn't looking at my watch. The time didn't matter. I know it wasn't long after I ate with my friends inside the hotel."

"Well, what time was that?"

Rosemary sighed. "I don't know. Let's see — we came down from Alex's room at five thirty and then after a bit we split up to get food and a bottle of wine that the porter carried in for us. We met up in the small lounge down the hall from the lobby and sat by the fireplace to eat. We stayed there a while, talking. I guess it was about seven when we came back out into the courtyard. And then we weren't out here long before I saw Mitch talking to some man and we all went over to join them."

Langford stopped writing and looked up. "Who was he talking to? Do you have a name?"

Rosemary scrunched up her forehead in thought. "Uh, Denny something. He's an attorney in private practice. Denny . . . Rivers! That's it. I remember because I pictured him in a canoe. I always try to think of something visual to remember names."

Langford nodded. "Okay, good. So, you met up with Mitch and Denny about seven. Then what?"

"Denny left right away because we were there. The five of us talked to Mitch for a few minutes and then I offered to sit with him while he got his dinner and ate, and my friends left. Mitch and I sat and talked for a while after he finished eating and then we danced to a couple of numbers. Then, a couple of people I didn't know came along and talked to him, so I left to look around for my friends. That was probably eight thirty, as a guess."

"Did you find your friends?"

"No. There were too many people and I was in no hurry, anyway, as they were all together. I did run into a couple of Goddesses."

Langford put down his pen. "Goddesses?"

Rosemary stifled a chuckle. "I'm a member of the Mystic Goddesses — the society who sponsored this ball."

Langford nodded and put the pen to paper again. "And what are their names?"

Rosemary shrugged. "Honestly, I only knew they were Goddesses because they were in costume and wearing masks. There are over a hundred members in the Society and I don't know them all. I recognized one of the girls. Her name is Sophie. I don't know her last name. I think she called another one 'Sue.' We were just chatting about the party, that the band was great — that kind of thing."

"So, when did you find your college friends?"

"They found me while I was talking to those Goddesses."

"What time was that?"

Rosemary sighed. "I really don't know. I guess about an hour after I had last seen them — so that would be nine-thirty or so. Not long after that the hotel manager got up on the stage and called for a doctor. We all followed after them to see what was going on, and we saw . . . we saw that someone was on the ground . . . and then we saw Mitch's red tartan kilt sticking out."

Langford sat still as Rosemary put her head down and sobbed.

After a minute, she looked up and patted her eyes with bits of torn tissue. "Why are you asking me all these questions about where *I* was and what *I* was doing all evening when I don't even know what happened to my husband. Do you know what killed him?"

Langford put down the pen and closed the notebook. "Yes, I know *exactly* what killed your husband. He was fatally poisoned with potassium cyanide that someone put in his drink."

Rosemary's mouth dropped open. "What? But that's crazy! Who would do such a thing? And at this party?"

Langford folded his arms across his chest. "Why don't you tell me about your marriage, Ms. Stuart."

Rosemary stared at the detective for several seconds, seeming to turn things over in her mind before she answered. Finally, she said, "I wasn't happy in my marriage because I believed my husband was being unfaithful to me. I'm telling you the truth because I had *nothing* to do with poisoning him, and I don't know anyone who would. He was someone who made friends easily. I never knew him to have any enemies, except people he put in prison, I suppose." Her eyes filled again with tears she dabbed at uselessly with the shredded tissue.

Langford waited a few moments. "I appreciate your honesty, Ms. Stuart. I would have found out about your marital troubles anyway, but I'm glad you volunteered the information. And I'd like to believe that you had nothing to do with poisoning your husband. You're a beautiful woman and you seem like a nice person. Unfortunately, you can't be eliminated as a suspect at this time, since you had both opportunity and motive."

"I have nothing to hide, Detective. I don't even know where I would get — what was it? — potassium cyanide. And, as you see, I don't have a purse where I could hide anything like that."

Langford glanced at her outfit. "You have a large pocket in that jacket."

Rosemary patted it. "Right, and I'll gladly show you what's in it." She grabbed at the green fabric and feathers sticking out. "Here's my mask, then my driver's license, a lipstick, my ticket for the ball, and . . . what the hell is this?" She held up a clear bottle with an aspirin label on the front with some white compound in the bottom.

The detective quickly reached into his case and pulled on a pair of latex gloves.

"Looks like a bottle of aspirin. Here, I'll take it." With two fingers he twisted off the cap and smelled inside while Rosemary looked on, wide-eyed.

When he tipped the bottle, white crystals came out onto his forefinger. He brought his finger up to his tongue, then puckered his lips at the taste. Brushing off the powder, he replaced the cap. Reaching down into his case again, he brought out a small paper bag and slipped the bottle into it, returning the bag to his case.

Slowly, he turned to face Rosemary. "I think the word is 'bingo.' Looks like you were able to find the potassium cyanide after all. It was right there in your pocket."

Chapter 17

ROSEMARY HELD HER FACE in her hands, vigorously shaking her head. "You can't think *I* put that cyanide bottle in my pocket. And then, what — pulled it out right in front of you? How dumb do you think I am?"

He smiled benignly. "It could have been a very smart move. You knew you had the cyanide bottle in your pocket and realized you'd be searched by the police who would find it, making you look guilty as hell. Whereas, if you *innocently* pulled it out of your pocket in front of the detective, it would appear to have been planted. How am I doing?"

Her shoulders slumped. "So, if I took it out of my pocket, or if I didn't take it out of my pocket, I'm equally guilty. It's a lose/lose situation for me. I can't prove a negative."

Langford gave her an eye roll. "You're breaking my heart. Look, before you get all soppy about this, did you notice that I put on gloves to handle the bottle and then carefully put it in a paper bag?"

Her face cleared. "Yes, so?"

"So, I didn't make detective for being able to jump to conclusions. I put on gloves to preserve *any other* prints that may be on it. We already know yours are all over it, thanks to your little show of emptying your pocket. The CSI people will dust it and pick up any other prints as well as yours that we'll have as an exemplar. For your sake, I hope we'll get a clear print from someone else."

Rosemary sat up straighter. "Then you can run the print through your database and hopefully find a match."

"Yeah, right. Unfortunately, this isn't 'Forensic Files.' If the perp isn't in the database, then we need a suspect to compare prints to, or the prints maybe were wiped off, or they're too smudged to identify. Let me ask you this — do you have any thoughts on how that aspirin bottle could have ended up in your pocket? Who had the opportunity?"

Rosemary fell back against her chair. "Good question. I was only with my friends and Mitch—except walking past a lot of strangers in the courtyard when someone could have dropped it in my pocket without me noticing." She stared off into space. "I dunno. That seems pretty farfetched, but nothing makes any sense. I wouldn't have believed anyone would kill Mitch, but someone did. And then, Mitch and I were in disguises, so only a few people close to us could identify us and why would any of them want to kill him and implicate me?"

Langford nodded. "Now, you're seeing how the process of elimination works . . . and why you'd be the prime suspect in anybody's book; but everyone else has to be eliminated. There's a famous line from Sherlock Holmes that goes, 'When you have eliminated the impossible, whatever remains, however improbable, must be the truth'."

Rosemary sighed. "I know the quote, but this isn't a detective story; it's my life. My husband has been cruelly murdered by some monster and you think *I'm* that monster."

Langford pressed his lips together in thought. "Actually, I don't think you are. I'm a pretty good judge of character but, more importantly, you're too obvious. I find it hard to believe you'd keep the bottle of poison on your person. You would've dropped it in the nearest trash can. And, if your friends corroborate your story that you were with some Goddesses on the other side of the fountain at least five minutes before your husband was poisoned, it's unlikely that you could have done it. Let me ask you this— is it *possible* that Mitch could have taken his own life?"

Rosemary swung around to face him. "Absolutely not. He had a good life. He loved being the county District Attorney. He was well-known and he was respected; even feared. Also, he never showed any signs of clinical depression or undue stress. I'm a school counselor, so I'm used to recognizing those warning signs in children. Mitch was always upbeat and positive. He wouldn't have ended his life like that. And without leaving a note? Please. He would have left a dissertation."

Langford smiled. "Okay, I'll consider Mitch committing suicide as being improbable. How about your friends? They had opportunity and they were among the few who knew your husband's disguise. I'd bet that you told them you were unhappy in your marriage. That your husband was cheating on you."

Rosemary hung her head. "Yes, of course I did, but it's not possible one of them killed Mitch. Not just because they're decent, good people; they would literally be the last people on earth to plant evidence to implicate me. Besides, I told them right before we came downstairs for the ball that I was going to find an attorney to file for a divorce and get on with my life. And they could see that I was in a good mood and looking forward to the evening."

Langford stretched out his legs and folded his arms. "Okay, you're certain they can be eliminated. I'm not convinced, but I'll be interviewing them and see what I come up with. Let's move on. Did Mitch ever mention he had convicted any of the Goddesses — or their family members — of any crimes? They would have had opportunity and motive."

Rosemary shook her head. "He never told me about any Goddess he tried, but he might have kept that to himself, and he probably wouldn't have known about family members or friends. As I told you, there are over a hundred women in the society and I don't even know every member; or many of them very well."

"That's understandable." Langford looked out into the crowd and sighed. "There are like two hundred people out there who had opportunity to commit this crime and one of them had motive — maybe more than one." He turned to look at Rosemary. "Y'know, I could go easy on myself and simply arrest you on probable cause right now. But I'm going to interview everyone who could have a motive, or who might have seen something. I *will* need you to come down to the station and sign a statement with another detective."

"You mean, tonight?"

"Oh — I'm sorry. Is that inconvenient?" Langford asked, dryly.

Rosemary muttered something under her breath before saying, "Can I just go upstairs and change out of this first? I don't think I can drive in this dress and I'm wearing a crown. My regular clothes are upstairs in my friend's room."

Langford covered his laugh. "I think that's acceptable. I'll have Sharon, the CSI, escort you upstairs. She needs to take your prints, anyway. Stay here and I'll get her. Then I'll talk to your friend, Alex."

"Please, go easy on her," Rosemary pleaded. "She's a good friend and she's got nothing to do with this."

Langford made a show of smoothing his hair and straightening his lapels. "Oh, I'll be charm itself. I mean, I wouldn't want to upset her."

Chapter 18

AS LANGFORD WAS MAKING his way through the crowd back to the CSI team, Betsy Davis waved him down and fell in step. "I'm glad I ran into you, Detective. I was just thinking, with all these police and investigators around, if I make an announcement asking the couple who reported the sick guest to report to the lobby, they might get scared off and leave the hotel and we'll never know who they are."

Langford glanced sideways at her. "You have a better idea?"

"Yes, I think so—if you agree. I remembered that they both had on leopard-print masks. I haven't seen any others like that, so I don't think they'd be too hard to identify. And since all my housekeepers and porters are working tonight – setting out food, bartending, keeping the area picked up and whatnot, I could send them out to look everywhere so we wouldn't miss them."

Langford nodded. "Okay, that's fine. But if they don't find the couple in the next, say, fifteen/twenty minutes, use the microphone. Those two are potential witnesses to whoever put the cyanide in the victim's drink."

"I understand. I'll check back with you."

Langford stopped in his tracks. "Betsy, you've reminded me of something else you can help me with. I'm going to need the names of everyone who's here tonight. Since people had to buy a ticket, there must be a list; and some must have just walked in, uninvited, so I'll need everyone to leave by the front door. I'll get a couple of uniforms to stand by the other exits, but I'd like you to contact whoever is in charge of the guest list to be prepared to sit by the front door to check off names and add others. I'll meet with her and offer assistance from the department if she needs it. Can you hunt up whoever's in charge?"

Betsy nodded and checked her watch. "It's about eleven and the party goes on until midnight —to the last minute of Mardi Gras — but some people will leave early, so I'll find the chairperson right away."

"Good. I'll get the two officers who are here to report to the other exits."

Langford continued on to the crime scene. After meeting briefly with the officials there, the two uniformed policemen headed off on their assignments and he and Sharon walked back to where Rosemary waited. After making the introductions, he said to Sharon, "I'll use the mic to summon Ms. Stuart's friends to get the room key and then I'll want to interview all of them, individually."

Five minutes later the four women were trailing the detective back from the bandstand to meet with Rosemary and Sharon.

Millie handed Rosemary her key. "Here you go, sweetie. Detective Langford told us you need to change clothes to go down to the station to sign a statement. How are you doing? Are you okay?"

Rosemary's lower lip began to tremble. "Not really, but I'm hanging in there. Thanks."

"She's doing fine," Langford added. "Sharon will be with her and give her whatever assistance she needs. Now, if y'all are ready. I'd like to ask you a few questions about what you heard and saw tonight." He glanced over at Alex. "I'll see you first — Ms. Trotter, is it? — and then the rest of you ladies." He tilted his head towards the Inn. "Let's go inside and find someplace where we can hear ourselves think."

Rosemary turned to Sharon. "Can I see my husband before I leave? They'll probably be taking him to the hospital before I get back."

Sharon looked at Langford for an answer. "We're done with the scene, Detective."

He shrugged. "Yeah, okay. You can see him, but don't touch the body."

Rosemary's eyes brimmed with tears. "I promise I won't touch him." Sharon put an arm around her and turned to lead her away as the others looked after them.

Langford cleared his throat to bring the attention back to himself. Glancing around at the four women he said, "Okay, ladies, let's go in. This shouldn't take too long."

Chapter 19

LANGFORD USHERED Alex into the unoccupied lounge and gestured to one of the loveseats. As she sat and arranged her full skirt around her, he pulled up a nearby chair.

"Okay, Ms. Trotter." He brought out his notebook, opened it, and turned to a page which he scanned before looking up. "Uh, Ms. Davis already gave me your home address and cell phone number and such. She said you arrived on Sunday afternoon. So, you drove down from Atlanta?"

Alex nodded. "I did. It's just a five-hour drive, mostly on the interstate. I was the first one of our group to arrive — actually, an hour earlier than I thought, with the time change."

"I've been told by Ms. Stuart that this was a ten-year reunion of your little group from Woodley College. Is that right?"

"Yes. We became friends as freshmen when we lived in the dorm, and then we and other friends moved to an off-campus house for the last two years."

Langford stroked his chin and gazed out the window. "It's only a five-hour drive from Atlanta, and yet, you hadn't visited Ms. Stuart any other time during these ten years?"

Alex was momentarily taken aback by the innuendo in his question. "I lived in Chicago until last year when I got married . . ." she paused and held his gaze for a moment, "to a homicide detective."

Langford's eyebrows rose. "Really."

"Yes. My husband's name is Arlie Tate. I use my maiden name for business purposes. I'm a tour operator. I call my service, Globe-Trotter Travels."

"Clever. Did you meet your husband on one of your trips?"

"You could say that. Someone in my group was murdered on Bedford Island, South Carolina. Arlie was a detective in nearby Saint Annes then and was called in to investigate.

Langford was leaning back, chewing on the end of his pen. "Hmmm. That's not one of those 'cute-meets,' is it? Well—I have to ask— did your husband solve the murder?"

"Actually, *I* did. But it was Arlie who came to the rescue in the end."

"How romantic. And people continued to sign up for your tours after one of your clients had been murdered?"

"Of course. Not that I advertised it, but I wouldn't deny it either. To tell you the truth, unfortunately, there have been other murders on my tours."

Langford started. "*Other* murders? Like, how many?"

Alex looked down at her nails and buffed them on her skirt. "Only a few. . . out of many trips. Besides, it wasn't always one of my clients who was murdered."

Langford pointed his pen at her. "Let me guess. Sometimes, one of your clients was the killer."

Alex pressed her hands against her cheeks. "Look, Detective, the only reason I brought up any of this is to let you know that I've had some success at being an amateur sleuth. If my husband were here, he'd tell you that I have good instincts for homing in on a suspect. In fact, I think I could be in a position to help you — if I knew more about what happened to Mitch."

Langford leaned back and crossed his arms. "I haven't even eliminated *you* as a suspect. Before you get all 'Agatha Christie' on me and take charge of the case, do you mind if I ask a few questions?"

Alex held back her smile. "Sure. Go ahead."

"All right. Rosemary told me she discussed her marital problems with you; that she thought her husband had been cheating on her. Can you see how that could give you a motive to get him out of the way, to do her a favor?"

Alex waved away the question. "As you pointed out, Detective, I haven't seen Rosemary in ten years, and I never even met Mitch before last night when we all had drinks and dinner with him. And then, he was quite charming. Just before the ball, Rosemary told us she planned to see an attorney for a trial separation or divorce. She was in the best mood we've seen her in since we got here. She loved being dressed up in her costume as a queen. We were all enjoying ourselves until we saw Mitch lying there on the ground . . . and then learned he had died."

Langford looked up from his writing. "Speaking of that, how long was Rosemary with y'all before you saw the body?"

Alex looked off into space. "Let's see. The four of us were looking for her for a while, and then we saw her with a group of Goddesses dressed as show girls or something. After we got her attention, she left them and joined us and shortly after that we heard Betsy on the PA system asking for a doctor. I guess it was about five minutes from the time we saw her."

Langford nodded. "That corroborates her alibi — but you two were together after the body was found, so you could have gotten your stories together."

"We didn't know then that Mitch had been murdered. I *still* don't know how he was killed."

"No reason not to tell you now. Somebody put potassium cyanide in his drink."

Alex looked at him wide-eyed.

"And the bottle containing the poison turned up in your friend Rosemary's pocket."

Alex fell back against the sofa. "Oh, my God! That's impossible. I mean — that she poisoned Mitch. Somebody had to have planted the bottle on her. Rosemary was in total shock when we heard Mitch had some kind of attack and died. I could tell if she was faking it."

"You haven't seen her in ten years. She might have honed her acting skills."

Alex vigorously shook her head. "She's the same person I knew for four years and she's no killer."

Langford sat back and laced his fingers behind his head. "Okay, let's assume that neither of you killed the guy. *Somebody* out there did. How would you help me figure out who it was?"

"Okay . . . good question."

"Thanks."

Alex took in a deep breath and slowly exhaled. "Look, I'm staying here until Friday and I'll be spending a lot of time with Rosemary until then. She must hold the key to who would have a motive to kill Mitch, even if she doesn't know it yet. Unless there's some psychopath out there who's managed to fit in as a party guest, it must be someone in their social circle who had a reason to want to see him dead; maybe, someone whose relative he sent to prison. I could pick Rosemary's brain to come up with some names to check out."

Langford shrugged. "Okay. I can see that you might be able to get Rosemary to remember something pertinent, or if she can pick up some gossip from her Mystic group; whatever. Then, you let me know and I'll do the investigating. I want to make that clear. It's fine if you can come up with a theory or a name to be checked out, but I'll take it from there."

Alex pressed down on the pleat on her skirt. "I hear you, Detective, but I can't predict what I'll find out or what suspects may show up out of the blue."

Langford leaned forward. "I mean it, Alex. We're talking about a cold-blooded killer here who's also a coward by the method that was used to take someone's life. I don't want to be responsible for you confronting this fiend who wouldn't hesitant to do the same to you."

Chapter 20

LANGFORD SHOOK his head ruefully as he watched Alex leave the lounge to call in one of her friends for the next interview. Her nonchalant attitude about uncovering potential suspects had left him unnerved. Hopefully, she would heed his advice and not pry into Stuarts' relationships other than securing a couple of names of people who may have had run-ins with the deceased. Her belief that the killer must have known Stuart well had merit, and Rosemary likely would have heard the person's name. Anyway, he hadn't identified any possible suspects other than Rosemary, and he didn't really think she had poisoned her husband at a Mardi Gras party in front of a couple hundred potential witnesses.

He spent the next half hour meeting with the other four other women, in turn, taking specific notes on their activities at the ball. Their accounts were all similar, with slight differences in times that gave them more credibility as it indicated they hadn't gotten together to constructed a story with a timeline that would protect Rosemary.

After concluding his last interview with Josie Higgins, who had impressed him with her accurate recollections and forthright testimony, he felt assured that none of the women had anything to do with the murder of Mitch Stuart. Gazing out the window at the crowd walking by, blithely talking and laughing, he could only wonder who did.

Glancing at his watch, he saw it was getting close to midnight when the party would end and everyone would be going home — and no longer be available for questioning. He fantasized that maybe, if he stood by the front door and made eye contact with everyone as they were leaving, he'd be able to identify the killer by observing a guilty look.

Leaving the lounge, he walked with a heavy step back to the lobby. As he entered the crowded room, he noticed Betsy Davis waving at him to get his attention, so he headed over to the reception desk.

"There you are, Detective. I've been waiting for you to finish your interviews with the young ladies to tell you my housekeeper, Maria, found the couple in the leopard masks who reported Mr. Stuart's seizure. They're sitting on the sofa over there, waiting to speak with you. I see they took off their masks. They're the ones in the orange outfits — who are looking at us right now." Betsy smiled at them and fluttered her fingers. "Their names are"—she glanced down at a notepad —"John and Camelia Burton."

"Good work, Ms. Davis . . . or, good work by Maria." He nodded at the couple and held up a finger to indicate he'd be with them momentarily.

He first wanted to check out the activity at the front door. Looking in that direction, he was pleased to see a woman sitting at a table, flipping through a sheaf of papers and appearing to make check marks as she stopped people who were about to leave. Langford had to smile at her outfit — a light blue pinafore with a white puffy-sleeved blouse underneath. Her dark hair was pulled back in braids. He couldn't see her feet, but he had no doubt that she was wearing spangled red shoes.

Glancing over to see that the Burtons were still waiting for him, he quickly slipped past a group who had stopped to talk, and approached the woman at the front door. "Hi. I'm Detective Drew Langford, and you're—?"

"Dorothy Gale." Her face, dotted with drawn-on freckles, crinkled into a grin. "I'm sorry — I couldn't resist. I know this is a serious business. My name is Joan Callahan. I was told that you needed to account for everyone who's here tonight, so I'm checking off names. So far, I've had good luck with finding them . . . but people have only started leaving. I can't believe that one of our guests could have drugged someone."

He shrugged a non-response. "I just stopped by to see how it's going and if you'd feel more comfortable with an officer here."

She shook her head. "I think I'm fine. I was told to just tell people I'm checking names for who to invite next year. That way, no one'll get upset. Anyway, the hotel manager's here and there are lots of Mystic members around to help out. Ms. Davis said she'd relieve me in a little while to finish up and that she'd get a copy of the list to you."

"Okay, very good. Thanks for doing this, Ms. Callahan. Just be sure you write down any names that aren't on the list, too."

"Sure. Of course."

He smiled briefly, then turned and crossed over to the sofa and introduced himself to John and Camelia Burton. He noted that the couple was leaning into each other with tensed shoulders. Langford gestured to the hallway behind the reception desk. "Please follow me down that hall to the lounge where we can have a little privacy."

The two glanced at each other before getting to their feet.

Langford attempted a breezy tone. "This won't take long. I just need to fill in a few gaps."

The Burtons followed him down the hall until they came to the lounge where Langford led the way in and invited the couple to take one of the loveseats while he sat in the nearby chair. Stretching out his legs, he pulled out his notebook and clicked a ballpoint pen. "So. Ms. Davis tells me you were good enough to seek her out to get help for one of the guests who appeared to be in distress."

John and Camelia turned to each other and smiled, looking more relaxed. John Burton said, "Yes, we found her as soon as we could."

"Very good. What I'd like to hear from you is exactly how you came to notice Mr. Stuart — the man having the seizure; where you were in relation to him, and what all did you see him do."

John looked over at his wife who nodded encouragingly. "Okay," he took in a breath and let it out. "We had just gotten drinks at the outside bar and were walking around looking for an empty table to sit down for a few minutes."

Langford nodded as he wrote, then glanced up waiting for him to continue. "Uh, I first noticed that the man you say is Mr. Stuart was sitting alone, so I wondered if he was waiting for someone to join him, or if he was about to get up if maybe someone had just left."

"How close were you to Mr. Stuart when you first saw him?"

Burton glanced at his wife. "At first, he was, what? — maybe twenty feet away."

"Okay, did you walk up closer to him?"

"Yes, as I said, we wanted to know if he was about to leave, so we started over towards him to ask."

"Excuse me, when you were looking at him, did you see Mr. Stuart take a drink?"

"Yes. When I saw him drain his drink, I figured he was probably about ready to leave."

"You didn't notice anyone nearby, maybe walking away, who could have been with Stuart just before he finished his drink?"

"No. When we heard later that the man may have been drugged, Cammy and I tried to remember if we noticed anyone who could have been with him, but neither of us could. Of course, there were a lot of people around, but we didn't see anyone speak to Mr. Stuart. Anyway, I was just about to ask him if he was leaving when he grabbed at his shirt collar and gasped for air. His face turned beet red."

Langford looked up. "Did he say anything then?"

"No, he just made choking sounds."

"Where were you then?"

"We were, like, next to him. I asked him if I could get him something, thinking maybe an epi-pen if he was having an allergic reaction."

Langford rubbed his temple. "But he didn't say anything. Did he seem to look at anyone, or point to anyone?"

"No. I'd say that he couldn't understand what was happening to him, that he was in shock. Then he went into convulsions, I'd say, and Cammie and I ran off to find the manager, thinking she should call for help. We found her at the reception desk and she came out with us. She immediately called for an ambulance. After the EMT people arrived with the police, no one was allowed in the area, so we went into the Carriage House bar and listened to the band there — just to shake off the nerves from that experience."

"Who told you Mr. Stuart had been drugged?"

"That was the scuttlebutt. When the housekeeper, Maria, found us and said you wanted to see us, we were afraid we should have done more to help Mr. Stuart, but . . . "

Langford waved off the remark. "No, there was nothing you could have done. You're not in any trouble. You did fine. I forgot to ask, but had you seen Stuart with anyone earlier in the evening?"

Camelia spoke up. "I remember seeing him with a lady in a purple dress who was wearing a crown. I noticed both their costumes, but his in particular because he was wearing a kilt, so he stood out."

Langford's eyes narrowed. "How much earlier?"

"Oh, like an hour before that. Mr. Stuart appeared to be eating at the time."

Langford sighed and made an entry in his notebook. "Thanks, folks. That'll be all. Please go down to the station at 320 Dauphin Street tomorrow and sign a statement. One of the detectives will be expecting you."

Chapter 21

AFTER THEIR INTERVIEWS, the four women got together to go out and stroll around the courtyard. Exiting the inn, they were struck by how lovely the area still looked with its strings of colored lights overhead and the amber pools of illumination around the shrubbery and on the pathways. But the atmosphere had changed from celebratory to somber. Two of the inn's housekeepers, filling in as waitresses, were picking up empty plastic glasses from the last few stragglers at the tables. The bartenders were packing up bottles of liquor to return to the Carriage House. Band members were observed putting away their instruments and high-fiving one another after their long night's work.

Alex pointed to a table with four chairs near the fountain, in view of the bar. "Let's sit there and talk for a few minutes. I think we're all too keyed up to go to bed now, anyway."

Once seated, they looked at one another for several seconds without speaking. "I know," Alex said, breaking the silence, "this was probably the worst Mardi Gras party in the history of the world."

Millie shrugged. "For a while it was great — dancing and eating and drinking . . . and then someone killed Mitch. It reminds me of that old joke, 'Besides that, Mrs. Lincoln, how did you like the play?'"

Dottie snickered. "I still don't know what happened. I mean, what's being investigated? Does Detective Langford know what killed Mitch? He didn't tell me anything in my interview. He just asked me about our movements during the evening and what time it was when we hooked up again with Rosemary before we heard her husband had had an attack and died."

"I wasn't told anything, either," Josie put in. "I figured I wasn't a suspect, so I just answered as accurately and with as much detail as I could."

"I'm sure you did," Alex said with a little smirk. "I guess I was nosier than you guys. I up and asked Langford what had killed Mitch. I thought that knowing what it was might help me remember something useful."

"So — what did he say?" Millie asked.

"He said Mitch was poisoned by potassium cyanide that had been put in his drink."

"Wow," Millie said under her breath.

"That's not all," Alex continued. "Rosemary found a bottle of the poison in her pocket when she was being interviewed. She says she has no idea how it got there." The other three looked furtively at one another. "Oh, c'mon, you know she didn't poison Mitch. Even Langford doesn't think that. Remember, she was with us when the doctor said Mitch drank the cyanide. It kills a person in three minutes."

Dottie clamped her hands on her face. "Oh, my God, this is terrible."

"It'd be much worse if Rosemary was the killer," Alex said. "I'm sure she's not, but *we* need to find out who is."

They stared at her. "Who — us?" Josie asked.

"Yes — us. We're all here until Friday, giving us two full days to solve the mystery. And we have the skills to carry this off. You're thorough and methodical, Josie. Millie is perceptive and intuitive; and, Dottie is positive and energetic. And I have some experience with forensics and police procedures."

"Yeah, we're regular 'Charlie's Angels,'" Millie cracked.

Josie lowered her eyes. "Jeez, I sound dull compared to the rest of you."

"You're not dull," Alex countered. "You're like Kate Jackson — the serious-minded, brainy one."

"So, who are you? Millie asked. "There were only three angels as I recall."Alex made a face. "I guess I have to be 'Bosley.' To finish the comparison, Langford will be Charlie. I've told him we'd work with Rosemary to come up with some names of possible suspects. It's hard to believe that she wouldn't have *some* inkling about a person who hated Mitch enough to kill him."

"What can we do besides that?" Dottie asked.

Alex splayed her hands on the table. "I'm glad you asked. Tomorrow, after breakfast, I thought we'd go over to Rosemary's and hammer out a plan. I have some ideas, but you all should think about it, too. One thing we need is a copy of the guest list. You noticed the woman at the front door dressed as Dorothy from the *Wizard of Oz*?" They nodded. "Well, she's checking off everyone's name as they leave. Betsy told me she'd make a copy for Rosemary to go over."

"That's a complete list of suspects." Millie said.

Alex nodded. "Yeah, but it's over two hundred people. Langford will run the names through the FBI data bank to look for criminal records. I think we'll have more luck with Rosemary who could recognize a name that doesn't belong there. Someone who snuck in. We'll see."

Dottie's face lit up. "This is exciting." She looked around guiltily. "I-I don't mean that it'll be *fun.* I mean, it's really terrible that Mitch was murdered."

Alex was gazing across the courtyard. "Yeah. I'm just thinking . . . Diego's over there taking down the bar. I wonder if he remembers when Mitch got his vodka tonic."

Josie started. "You don't want to accuse him of poisoning Mitch, do you?"

"No, of course not. He wouldn't know Mitch from a bar of soap. I just wonder if he saw anyone sitting with Mitch — who I'll describe as the 'guy wearing a kilt who got sick'."

Josie looked unconvinced. "Just be careful." She looked down at her watch. "Anyway, it's getting late. Maybe you want to wait 'til the morning?"

"No, I'd like to ask him now while the scene is unchanged. That could help him remember. You go ahead upstairs."

"I think we should go up, too," Millie suggested to Dottie.

"Sure. You all go up," Alex said. "I won't be long. See you upstairs, Josie. We'll all meet for breakfast, say about eight?"

"How about eight-thirty." Millie said. "Sounds like we'll be off and running the rest of the day."

Alex rolled her eyes. "Fine. Eight-thirty. See you then."

After they left, Alex walked over to where Diego was loading bottles into a carton. He looked up as she approached.

"Oh, hey, Diego. Sorry to bother you. I have a quick question. Um, I think you heard that one of the men at the party had an attack and was taken to the hospital."

Diego placed the last bottle into the box. "*Si*. I heard he died."

Alex nodded. "Yes he did. He was my friend's husband. I know he got a drink at your bar at about nine-thirty. Did you notice him and if anyone was sitting with him? He was wearing a Braveheart costume with a red plaid skirt."

Diego's forehead creased in confusion. "He was wearing a skirt?"

"The kind of skirt men wear in Scotland. A kilt."

Diego's face cleared. "Ah, *un falda escocesa. Si, si.* I did see a man who looked Scottish, but he was alone."

"Oh." Alex sighed in disappointedly. "Well, thanks, anyway, Diego. *Buenas noches.*"

She turned and walked around to the other side of the fountain to take another look at where Mitch had been found. The police tape had been removed, but she could still picture the scene as it was at the time. Looking around, she noticed there were no bushes nearby where someone could hide. How could the killer have had access to Mitch's drink? Diego said he didn't see anyone sitting with him, but someone could have stopped by briefly; someone Mitch knew who was able to distract him long enough to pour the cyanide into his glass.

Feeling the weight of the dilemma, she trudged over to the door that led into the west wing.

Upstairs, she tapped softly on the door to her room. Josie opened after a few seconds.

As she stepped inside, she squinted to try to see in the semi-darkness. "Is this enough light for you?"

"This is how I found the room," Josie explained. "Two of the lamps had been unplugged."

Alex stared at her. "Okay, now that's weird."

Chapter 22

"HI, ARLIE. IT'S ME," Alex said softly into her cell phone early the next morning.

"Why are you whispering?"

"Josie's not up yet, but I wanted to reach you before you left for work."

"I'm glad you did. I missed hearing from you yesterday. How was the Mardi Gras ball? I figured you were having such a good time you didn't have a chance to call."

"That's not exactly right."

"What part is wrong?"

"The part about the 'good time.' Rosemary's husband was fatally poisoned during the party."

"What?! Did Rosemary—?"

"No, I'm sure she had nothing to do with it, although she found the bottle of poison in the pocket of her outfit while she was being interrogated. Anyway, I'll give you more details later. We're all okay and Rosemary's home for now. I wanted to ask you a few things to help us get some information. I told Detective Langford that I'd try to come up with some possible suspects."

"Of course you did. What did Langford say to that?"

"He said it was fine to get names of people he could investigate, but I shouldn't confront anyone who could be the killer."

"That sounds reasonable; and I'm telling you the same thing. Promise me you won't take matters into your own hands. Do you want me to come down there to help out Rosemary?"

"No, there's no reason for that. The four of us will keep her company and see if she can figure out anyone who had any motive to kill Mitch. We think maybe one of the Goddesses could have taken revenge because Mitch sent a relative to prison. Can we get a list of the people who were convicted by the District Attorney in, like, the last six months?"

"I haven't checked out criminal procedures in Alabama — although I should have knowing that you always get involved in murder investigations wherever you go. I'm sure there's a law enforcement agency there that keeps all the criminal records; they allow public access to only some of them. What you could do is contact the Alabama Department of Corrections to get the names of all persons currently incarcerated."

Alex brightened. "Really? That's a great idea,"

"Well, I can see a problem with that. Unless the convict is the woman's husband, the last name won't be the same as the Goddess."

"Oh, yeah. It's too bad that Rosemary doesn't know many of the women in the society, to have heard much gossip."

"Maybe she knows someone in the group who has. Are you thinking a woman is the killer because poison is a woman's weapon?"

Alex paused a moment. "I guess I thought it's more likely than, say, if a knife were used to slit his throat."

Arlie chuckled. "Don't we have the nicest conversations? Anyway, you're right; since almost ninety percent of murders are committed by men, the fact that forty percent of poisonings are done by women, it's significant."

Alex gazed out the window. "Arlie, since we're on the subject, do you know where someone could buy potassium cyanide?"

"How close are they to a computer? You can buy it online. You should have to prove it's for an industrial purpose, but I doubt that online sales are regulated."

Alex blew air out between her lips. "Well, that's probably not worth checking into. Anyway, I know you need to get to work. Thanks for all the information, dear. And I'm sorry I didn't call you last night."

"I'm just as glad you didn't. I wouldn't have gotten any sleep. Call me whenever you can to let me know how it's going. And remember your promise to me and that Detective Langford, okay? Love you, babe."

"Love you, too." Alex hit the off button and slipped the phone into her pocket. After a minute, she walked over to the dresser to put on her makeup and brush her hair. Looking at herself in the mirror, she suddenly remembered something Mitch had said — something that could change the course of her investigation.

Chapter 23

ALEX DROVE HER SUBARU Forrester slowly down Government Street in the Oakleigh Garden Historic District of Mobile while the three passengers gaped out the windows at the mansions.

"Rosemary's must be that second one on the right," Millie announced, after confirming with the GPS.

Alex turned right into the driveway of the grey brick and stone French Renaissance Revival mansion and stopped halfway, in view of the carriage house in back. Turning off the ignition, she looked out her window for a moment to view the house with its pillared portico covering the entire façade. "Not a bad place to hang your hat. Rosemary never mentioned she lived in a French chateau." Over her shoulder, she added, "This is one of those places where the real estate listing reads, 'private showings for serious buyers only'."

Dottie chuckled. "It's beautiful, but it's so big for just two people."

"It's larger than Terrace House," Josie put in. "And there were twelve of us—thirteen with Dean Merrill."

Alex picked up her purse from the console. "Well, I guess we better go in and get to work. Everyone, take a deep breath. We have a big job ahead of us." She looked over at Millie. "Wouldn't it be fantastic if we could actually discover who murdered Mitch?"

Millie snickered. "'Who Murdered Mitch?'" sounds like the title of a cheap novel."

Alex lightly punched her arm. "Let's go. I'll open the back. Somebody grab Rosemary's dress."

As they all exited the SUV, Dottie came around to the back and gathered up the gown and crinolines and handed the crown to Josie before joining the other two on the stone path leading up to the house. At the wrought iron and glass doors, Alex pressed the doorbell which set off a sonorous version of Westminster's chimes that could be heard from deep inside. Millie turned and made a face. "Jeez, my doorbell only goes 'ding-dong'."

One of the two doors soon swung open revealing a dispirited-looking Rosemary who beckoned them inside. "I'm so glad to see you guys. I can't thank you enough for coming and offering to help."

"You could give us a cup of coffee," Millie suggested.

Rosemary smiled wanly. "I've got a full pot made — with some cookies to go with it."

Dottie held out the dress but her eyes were following the curve of the grand staircase up to the second floor. "I haven't seen a stairway like that since *Gone with the Wind.*"

"We're quite impressed with your house," Alex explained. "You could have saved us the price of admission to the Bragg-Mitchell plantation by showing us around here."

Rosemary shook her head. "I don't even think of this as *my* house. Mitch bought it for himself two years before we got married. I've always felt like a tenant here. It *is* a beautiful house, though. It was built in 1906, but it's had a lot of updating, of course, as you'll see. It's on a list of significant historical homes in Mobile. Anyway, let's go into the kitchen and get some coffee so Millie can settle down. Dottie, thanks for bringing the dress. I'll just put it in this hall closet for now."

Josie handed her the crown.

"Oh, thanks, Josie. Did you bring my scepter?" She glanced around at the others.

"Oh, oh. We forgot your scepter," Millie replied. "Can you get along without it today?"

Rosemary chuckled. "Hah! Funny. And I didn't think I'd find anything funny for a long time — not after last night."

Alex patted her shoulder. "Let's go get a cup of coffee and have you tell us first how it went at the station."

They followed Rosemary into the large modern kitchen that was lined with white cabinets that contrasted with the dark wood flooring and the rose and beige-colored granite counter.

Rosemary pointed to one corner. "The coffee's set up there with cups and cream and sugar. Help yourself. I thought we'd sit here in the breakfast nook."

After they were seated in the built-in banquette, Alex helped herself to a chocolate chip cookie. "So, you had to make a statement at the police station?"

Rosemary exhaled audibly. "Yes, I was taken back to one of those interrogation rooms where a female detective asked me some questions while videotaping me. Then, she had me write out what I had told Detective Langford. As I read it back, I thought to myself that *I* would have arrested whoever wrote it. I was the closest person to Mitch at the party and I had the bottle of poison. I can't believe they let me leave the station."

"You don't know how the bottle could have ended up in your pocket?" Josie asked, trying not to sound accusatory.

"No, but anyone in that crowded courtyard could have slipped it in my pocket without my noticing. The question is— *who*? Ever since last night I've been racking my brain to come up with anyone who would have known our disguises, had a motive to kill Mitch, and wanted to frame me. I'm drawing a blank on at least two of the three."

Alex put down her cup. "That's what we're here for — to figure out who it could be. You should know we all believe you're innocent — that you're not capable of killing anyone. Besides, you were with us when Mitch drank the poison. Right now, we need to dig up whatever we can to try to identify a suspect, so we'll need to pry into Mitch's and your business — if that's okay with you."

Rosemary stretched out her arms. "You can look anywhere and everywhere and ask me whatever you want to know. I have nothing to hide."

Alex rubbed her chin and studied the table for a minute. "Okay, I've come up with a theory as a basis for our investigation, but I'll need everyone's cooperation."

They all turned to look at her.

"This should be good," Millie said.

"Hear me out," Alex continued. "Okay, you've told us that you suspected Mitch was cheating on you."

"I thought so, but he denied it and I didn't have any proof; so, I don't know anymore. Right now, all I'm sure of is that he didn't deserve to die like that and I'm feeling guilty that I even joked about, y'know, 'knocking him off,' or something."

Josie shook her head. "You have nothing to feel guilty about — saying something in jest in the heat of the moment. And it's understandable that you're seeing him in the best light now after his death, but you told us he did things that made you suspicious, like staying away from home a lot without any explanation."

Millie tapped on the table. "If a man goes out at night and can't account for his time, he probably isn't practicing with the church choir."

Alex snickered. "Good point. But why I'm bringing this up again is to get into my theory of the crime and how we can go about solving it. Let me ask you this – what does my hair look like right now?"

Rosemary blinked. "What?"

"Just go along with me and I'll explain in a minute. How would you describe my hair: the style, color, whatever?" Alex turned her head from side to side and fluffed up the ends.

Rosemary shrugged. "Well, I'd say it's light brown with reddish highlights. It's a little longer than shoulder length and has soft, loose curls. You have good hair. Is that what you wanted to hear?"

Alex waved away her last comment. "You'll understand what I'm getting at after you answer another question. How would you have described my hair Sunday when we were at the parade; after being outdoors for, like, three hours."

Rosemary looked off into space. "Well, I think your hair had become all frizzed out and bushy, as I recall. I've seen it like that before when you're outside for very long. Are you going to ask me how your hair looks when you get up in the morning, too?"

"Uh, no. Actually, this is the end of the quiz. Now, let me take you back to Monday night when we were at Cyril's bar and Mitch came in and joined us. Remember how he made a little game of guessing who we were based on our appearances?"

Everyone nodded.

"Okay. When he came to me, he correctly called me by name, describing my hair as prone to frizzing up outside. He also said I had on a foreign-made sweater, which was perceptive. The point is, Monday night in the bar, my hair was just as it is now. It was lying flat because we had spent the day indoors visiting the museum and the Bragg-Mitchell house. Then, the four of us went back to the inn to relax before we had to get ready to meet you and Mitch for dinner. Did you ever tell Mitch that humidity frizzes up my hair?"

Rosemary stared blankly at her. "I'm sure I never told him that."

Alex's eyes shone in excitement. "Exactly. So, the only way he would have known that was by seeing me when I was with you at the parade, after we had been outdoors all evening."

Rosemary took up the narrative. "And when we saw *him* with the redhead who he said he just ran into and she was thanking him for letting her off."

Alex held up her hands like a magician. "It all came back to me this morning when I looked in the mirror. Mitch made up the story that he had just run into that woman *after he saw us at the parade*—or he would have told you he had seen you. I think he probably lied about a lot of other things, too. I remember you saying once that you felt you didn't really know him — and that brings me around to my theory."

"It's about time," Millie said under her breath.

"Okay, I deserved that," Alex agreed. "Now, hear me out. I had been thinking we should be taking a look at the people at the party — looking for a criminal record or that of a relative who Mitch prosecuted. Now, I think we should be taking a close look at *Mitch.* We need to find out a lot more about his activities and his relationships outside of his marriage. It's not likely that the redhead, Stacy Gibson, was his only extramarital affair. What if he had been sleeping with one of the women in your Society and then broke it off right before the ball? That could have been a motive to murder him and she'd have the opportunity to poison his drink."

Rosemary leaned forward. "How would we go about finding out more about someone who's dead when I couldn't find out much about him when he was alive?"

Alex nodded. "That's a good question. The answer is that you didn't go behind his back to check out what he told you. That's what we're going to do. For instance, he obviously knew some of the people we saw at Cyril's although he told you he never went there. From what we saw, he must have been a regular."

Dottie snapped her fingers. "Remember he said he didn't know Shirley, our waitress, but she acted like she knew him quite well."

"Right," Alex agreed. "And there was another waitress at the bar Millie and I saw whisper in his ear when he was walking back to our table. Also, I don't think he was having a heated conversation with Cyril about rambunctious kids outside. We need to talk to everyone at Cyril's and see what they knew about Mitch."

Rosemary leaned back against the bench. "I feel faint talking about all this. But how can we possibly track down all these people, get them to talk, and identify the murderer in only two days?"

"There are five of us," Millie reminded her. "So that's like ten days for one detective."

"Except we're not really detectives," Josie said. "Still, we could take a shot at it. How do you think we should go about this, Alex?"

"We need to split up and cover all the bases." She opened the folded pages she had with her and pushed them across to Rosemary. "This is the list of everyone who was at the ball. The killer must be on one of these five pages. I've gone over it looking for anyone we've heard of who has some connection with Mitch, but I couldn't find any. I thought you could check it against a directory of the personnel in the District Attorney's office."

"I could help Rosemary with that," Josie suggested. "I could call out the names on that list while she checks the directory. Then we could look through Mitch's desk, check his email and anything else we can get into. Rosemary could look through his checkbook to see if there are suspicious deposits or checks. Is that okay with you, Rosemary?"

"Sure. As I said, this is no time to keep any secrets. There's someone out there who needs to be identified and locked up for killing Mitch. Nothing else matters right now."

Alex clapped her hands together. "Bravo. That's how we all feel. I'm sure Detective Langford will go through Mitch's office, too, but he's occupied right now with putting names and fingerprints in data bases to see if he can make any connections."

"What would you like me to do?" Dottie asked.

"How about trying to find Stacy Gibson? Mitch said she works as a cleaning woman in some hotel. Hopefully, that's true. Usually, good liars use facts whenever they can so they don't need to remember everything they've said. Start calling the downtown hotels in Mobile and see if they have an employee by that name and maybe we'll get lucky."

Dottie saluted dramatically. "Aye, aye, Admiral. Anything else?"

"Yes — go online and pull up the Alabama Department of Corrections. Arlie said they can give us a list of everyone who's currently incarcerated. We might get a hit if the surname's the same as someone on our guest list."

"I had to ask," Dottie joked. "What are you going to be doing?"

"I thought Millie and I would pay a visit to the Public Defender's office today and talk to that Mr. Jenkins — the man who stopped by our table at

Cyril's. He wasn't surprised to see Mitch with a table full of women, so he might know something about girlfriends. Then we need to visit the District Attorney's office in Government Plaza."

Rosemary gave a little snort. "Now I feel like we should be hanging out a shingle." She glanced at her watch. "Well, it's about noon. I bought some things for sandwiches. Why don't we grab a bite now, and then we can spend the rest of the day on our assignments."

"Good idea," Alex agreed. "Let's plan on going to Cyril's for dinner so we can talk to the people there. How does that sound?"

Before anyone could answer, the shrill peal of a phone on the kitchen counter made them jump. Rosemary's eyes darted around the group as though looking for an explanation. "Who could that be? I wasn't expecting to hear from anyone."

"How about answering it," Millie suggested.

Rosemary stood on unsteady legs, walked over and picked up the receiver. "Hello? Oh, hi, Detective. Uh, yes, my friends are here. . . You do? What . . . Oh . . . Really. . . Okay, yes, I'll tell them. Thank you so much for calling."

Rosemary replaced the receiver and turned to face the others. "I guess you heard that was Detective Langford." She paused. "He said . . . they found a second print on the bottle containing the poison. Unfortunately, there wasn't a match in the database, but it can be used against any suspects. We need to find one."

Chapter 24

ALEX NEATLY PULLED the Subaru into a visitor parking space in the garage attached to the modern complex that housed the offices of both the District Attorney and the Public Defender.

As she gathered up her purse and notebook, she turned to Millie. "I'm as ready as I'll ever be. I only hope people are willing to talk to us. We don't have any authority to demand information."

"We have our feminine charms," Millie said. "If that doesn't work, we can always cry."

Alex laughed as they both exited the car. "Okay, that's our strategy."

Inside the building they had to weave their way through a stream of people in business suits, all carrying briefcases, all appearing to be in a hurry. Sidestepping three men walking abreast who were engrossed in conversation, Millie commented, "There must be a lot of crime in Mobile, if this place is any indication,"

"There are a lot of private law offices in this complex; not just criminal law," Alex replied. "In fact, the Public Defender's office is new here. Up until two years ago a judge would appoint a private attorney from a list of criminal defense lawyers to represent a defendant. Now, there's a Public Defender's office with about fifty employees."

"Well, aren't you a fount of information," Millie observed.

"I had to go online to get the address so I pulled up a couple articles on the new system. Look over there — there are some directories by that bank of elevators. Let's check them out and get our bearings."

At the glass-fronted boards, Alex quickly scanned the lists, mumbling names to herself until she found what she was looking for. "Ah, here are the Deputy Public Defenders. We want Harold Jenkins. He's in Room 601. Let's go up."

Getting off the elevator, they followed the arrow down to the end of a hallway and cautiously opened the frosted glass door bearing the stenciled name of the Deputy P.D.

In the simply furnished waiting room, two men in suits were reading over some papers while a woman in casual clothes spoke quietly to a small child drawing in a coloring book.

Millie pointed at the receptionist behind a plexiglass window. 'That glass is probably bullet-proof," she said out of the corner of her mouth.

The neatly coiffed, middle-aged woman looked up as they approached. "May I help you?" she asked in a tone that was all business.

Alex spoke up. "I hope so. We don't have an appointment, but we'd like to see Mr. Jenkins about something of vital importance. We won't take too much of this time."

"I'm sorry, but Mr. Jenkins is very busy and others are waiting for him, as you can see." She glanced out at the waiting room. "I can make an appointment for you for another day, if you wish."

Millie leaned in. "We need to talk to him about District Attorney Stuart's murder."

The woman's face lost all color. "Mr. Stuart was murdered?" Her hand went to her throat.

"Last night," Millie replied. "We're investigating the matter."

The flustered woman knocked a paper off her desk as she reached across to hit the button on her intercom. "Mr. Jenkins, two ladies are here to see you. They don't have an appointment, but I think you want to hear what they have to say. Yes . . . okay, I'll bring them back. Thank you."

She pointed to a nearby door. "Come through there and I'll take you back to the Deputy's office."

Inside, they followed her down a hallway to a closed door. She knocked and cracked it open.

"Come in," a man's voice said as the receptionist held the door open for Alex and Millie to enter.

"Mr. Jenkins," Alex started, recognizing the man she had seen at the bar. "Thank you for seeing us. By the way, we were at District Attorney Stuart's table at Cyril's Monday night when you stopped by."

Jenkins appraised them with raised eyebrows. "And you are—?"

"I'm Alex Trotter and this is Millie Townsend. We're friends of Rosemary Stuart. I don't know if you've heard, but Mitch Stuart was murdered last night at a Mardi Gras party at the Granada Inn. We were there—as guests of the Stuarts."

"Murdered! How? By whom?"

"That's what we're here to talk about," Alex responded. "May we sit down?"

Jenkins gestured toward the two chairs that faced his desk. "Sit."

As they did, Alex opened her notebook and fished a pen out of her purse. "I'm sorry you had to hear about this from us. The police may be withholding a public statement right now as they've just started their investigation. We can tell you that Mitch died from potassium cyanide someone put in his drink at the party."

Jenkins' eyes widened. "Jeez. I can't believe this. That's terrible. But why are *you* here to tell me all this?"

Alex edged forward on her seat and spoke confidentially. "I'm going to be upfront with you. The police are looking at Rosemary as a suspect. We know she didn't do it. She was with us when Mitch drank the poison in another part of the courtyard, but the police don't have anything more to go on. You know how they always look at the spouse first." She took a breath. "Anyway, Millie and I are trying to learn something about Mitch's social contacts to see if we can find a connection to someone who was at the party; someone who might want to see him dead."

"And you think *I* can help you? I'm sure I don't know anyone who would want to kill the man. We were never close. I only knew him through work. I was never with him socially."

"I understand," Alex said. "But when we were at Cyril's, you teased him about being with a lot of women — like more than usual — as though you had seen him with women, before. Do you remember saying that?"

Jenkins pulled back his shoulders and stretched. "Okay, I see what you're getting at. You think I know something about his relationships with women."

"We know that Mitch had girlfriends," Millie inserted, "but we don't know who they are. We think an extramarital affair could have led to his murder. Someone's husband could have found out and killed him, or he jilted some woman who decided to take revenge. Something like that. We were wondering if you could give us the names of any of these women. Of course, we would hold your information in complete confidence. Can you help us out?"

Jenkins rubbed his chin, considering. "Okay, you're trying to find other suspects to take your friend Rosemary out of the spotlight. I get that. Unfortunately, I don't know any names, but I can give you some leads, maybe. In strictest confidence, like you said."

Alex gripped the arm of her chair to contain her excitement. "Fair enough. We didn't hear anything from you. Now, what can you tell us?"

Jenkins rocked back with his fingers laced behind his head. "Well, I can tell you that Mitch had a reputation for flirting with women in the department — and maybe taking it further. He was making sexual comments all the time. He was a good-looking guy and a lot of women responded to him. Some didn't seem to appreciate his attention. I'm talking about a couple of the social workers and a trial coordinator here in the office. What bothered me was that he seemed to offer lighter sentences or reduced bail to good-looking women. I don't have personal knowledge that this was in exchange for sexual favors, but it had that appearance. And if true, that was a violation of his oath to the people of Mobile County and compromised the security of this community."

Alex looked up from her notes. "Did you ever see him with any of the female defendants outside of court?"

"I'd see him on occasion having a drink with a woman I thought I recognized as a former client of another Deputy P.D. But I'd see him out with other women, too, usually at Cyril's. I didn't know the guy was married until the other night when I stopped by your table. I thought one of the waitresses there was his current girlfriend."

Alex scratched her head. "Did others in your department comment on his unequal treatment of defendants? Was he ever disciplined for going easy on some defendants, or for sexual harassment of those in the department?"

Jenkins shrugged. "Not that I ever heard of, but you'd have to inquire at the D.A.'s office. I can tell you that it was common knowledge in the P.D. office that his prosecutions of women who were up on drug charges or prostitution were influenced by their looks. We had an expression around the office for those women: 'Too pretty for prison,' which made our defense a lot easier."

"Do you have any knowledge that he misused his power with other actions that could be seen as corrupt or improper?" Alex probed, looking hard at him.

"I know personally that he once refused to approve a search warrant on the house of one female drug dealer without cause."

Alex and Millie shared a look as Jenkins continued. "He once gave up the name of a confidential informant that put the guy's life in danger and resulted in the slowdown of the investigation." Jenkins shook his head. "I think the State Attorney General should have looked into his record and disciplined him, or worse. Mitch was the highest-ranking law official in Mobile County."

Millie wrung her hands. "Sounds like there's a lot more here than just identifying someone as a womanizer. It sounds like he very well could have traded his justice for sexual favors."

Jenkins nodded. "He could have, but I don't know that for a fact."

Millie persisted. "Do you know the names of any of these 'too pretty' defendants whom he let off?"

Jenkins shook his head. "No, but you can look at the case filings and see what women got off easy. A lot of them probably have gone back to dealing drugs or prostitution."

"Were these married women?"

"Well, I doubt that many of them were, but I'm sure they had some kind of relationships, if I see what you're getting at. Most of the hookers would have a pimp who may have wanted to knock off Mitch for cutting into his profits. If Mitch had an ongoing relationship with any of these women, he was probably giving them money; maybe even keeping them off the streets — if you want to look at the bright side."

Alex shook her head. "I can't believe that you're the only lawyer here who suspected Mitch's improper or illegal conduct. Have you talked to anyone else about this?"

"Only making a comment here or there, but not having a discussion, no. I assume many in the D.A.'s office noticed that twinkies were getting off light while the hard-bitten types were sent away for years."

Alex nodded. "We'll see what we can find out. Do you think Mitch could have been involved in any other illegal dealings?"

Jenkins scoffed, "That would follow, but I don't have any personal knowledge of that. Again, you need to talk to someone in the D.A.'s office, but they probably won't tell you much."

Millie and Alex shared a look. Millie asked, "Could we get a list of your office's cases or dockets or whatever?"

Jenkins nodded. "Sure. It's a public record. Tell Jean, my office administrator, that I said you can have a copy of the court calendar for a couple months going back if you want. She'd have the docket, too, with summaries of the cases with their findings and sentencing."

"Thanks," Millie said. "Right now, we just need names to compare with the guest list we have for the ball."

Jenkins nodded. "Whatever. Just don't say you heard anything from me. I know you want to help your friend, and I think Mitch deserves justice as well. Whatever I thought of the guy, I'm sorry he was murdered — and with poison, no less."

Alex rose from her chair. "We won't divulge the source of anything you've told us, but I think you may have helped us track down the killer."

Chapter 25

THE TWO WOMEN left the Public Defender's office with Millie weighed down with a shopping bag full of papers.

"Well, are you ready to go talk to people in the D.A.'s office now?" Alex asked.

"I guess so — if you don't think the murderer is in one of all these cases." She lifted up the bag. "What do you expect to get from the D.A.'s office? They'll probably be defensive about Mitch."

"They may be, but we need to get the names of defendants who were represented by private attorneys who could have had some reason to kill Mitch. Here, I'll get the elevator button. I see you've got your hands full."

"Hah. Hah. You get the next load."

Back down in the lobby, Alex scanned through the directory listings to find the District Attorney's offices on the second and third floors. "Here we go. Mitch Stuart's office is in Room 320."

Upstairs, as they entered the D.A.'s waiting room, they were struck by how much plusher it was than the Deputy Public Defender's. This room had natural light coming in from ceiling to floor windows. It was well-appointed with upholstered furniture, mahogany tables, and original oil paintings making it look more like a hotel lounge than the office of a civil servant. The thick carpeting underfoot muffled the conversation of the two men in dark business suits who sat together going over documents spread out on briefcases on their laps.

Alex crossed over to the receptionist whose head jerked up when she approached. "Oh! I didn't hear you come in." The woman looked around as though someone else might be lurking close by to surprise her. "We've had a terrible shock today and I guess I'm on edge. Can I help you?"

"Well, uh, we'd like to speak to one of Mitch Stuart's staff members, or an Assistant District Attorney about —"

"Mr. Stuart's been murdered!" the receptionist blurted out.

Alex took a step back and held up a hand. "I know. That's what we came to talk about."

"Who are you?"

"My name's Alex Trotter and my friend, over there, is Millie Townsend. We're old friends of Rosemary's."

"Who?"

"Rosemary Stuart — Mr. Stuart's wife, er, widow. She's been questioned as a suspect in his murder, but we have proof she's innocent. We're here to find out if any of Mr. Stuart's recent convictions could be connected with his murder."

The receptionist cupped her hand around her mouth. "You think so? I overheard some of the Assistant D.A.s talking like that, too."

"Could we speak with one them?" Alex asked.

"Oh, I don't know. I think it'd be better if you talked to Mr. Stuart's paralegal, Marsha Grayson. I'll see if she can meet with you. She can get one of the Assistant D.A.s, if necessary. Why don't you have a seat while I check."

A few minutes later a plump young woman wearing horn-rimmed glasses came through the door carrying a thick file folder, and called out Alex's name.

Alex and Millie followed her back to a small conference room. The paralegal sat at one end of the table and gestured to sides of the table. "Please sit," she instructed as she pulled a stack of papers from her folder.

Alex and Millie pulled out chairs on the same side of the table and waited while the paralegal flipped through her papers. Ms. Grayson looked at them without speaking for several seconds. "I've been told that you've come here to get some information about defendants in our office on behalf of Mr. Stuart's wife who's a suspect in his murder."

Alex nodded. "Yes. We went to school with Rosemary Stuart. We can vouch for her character, and she was with us at the time Mr. Stuart was poisoned. But she's the only suspect the police have right now. We think the murderer could be someone who was convicted by this office — or a relative. We have a list of the people who were at the party that we could compare with any names you may be able to give us."

Ms. Grayson looked down at her papers. "You would have to agree that anything I tell you will be held in the strictest confidence. What I have here" — she tapped her file —"is not part of the public record, although the case names are. I've agreed to see you on behalf of Ms. Stuart. I'm sure she's distraught over her husband's murder, and then to be facing scrutiny by the police as well as others who suspect her makes it even worse. I think the only decent thing I can do is to share some information with you that could point to someone else being his killer."

Millie and Alex glanced at each other, then looked back to the paralegal.

Ms. Grayson squared her shoulders. "Again, anything I say is in strict confidence. I don't want you to use my name as the source of what I'm about to disclose."

Alex and Millie both nodded. "We can promise you that," Alex replied, leaning forward in expectation.

The paralegal fanned through the pages in front of her. "I've collected this material from the time I started working here a little over a year ago. Except for this unusual circumstance, all of this should have first been presented to the Assistant D.A.s for their review to decide whether to file a complaint with the State Attorney's office. If this material had been verified, it would have meant that Mr. Stuart could have lost his law license, or have even been sent to prison." She looked at the ceiling and swallowed. "I didn't think he would be *murdered* . . . and he might not be the only one here to be targeted," she finished, her voice taking on an edge.

Alex leaned forward, resting her hands on the table. "Do you have an idea of someone who may have killed Mr. Stuart?"

The paralegal squirmed in her chair. "I can't say that. And it isn't just one person I could point to as a possible suspect. Mr. Stuart's history of misconduct that I'm alleging has hurt a lot of people." She drummed her fingers on the papers in front of her. "Since I heard about the murder this morning, I've thought about just what you've said — that one of these defendants, or a relative, may have murdered him."

Alex tilted her head toward the file. "We appreciate any leads that you have there to compare with the list of guests; to find a connection, if not the same name."

The paralegal nodded. "Okay, if we're in agreement that this is confidential and only to be used by you to connect to the guest list and, if appropriate, to refer to the police to investigate, let's get started. What I'm thinking are the most likely cases that could lead to someone seeking revenge are convictions due to Brady violations. Do you know the supreme court case of Brady v Maryland?"

Alex nodded. Millie shook her head. "What did Maryland do?" she asked.

"The Maryland State Court of Appeals upheld the conviction of a man after it was learned that the prosecution possessed a written confession from the guy who was with Brady at the time of the murder. The Supreme Court ruled that the prosecution is required to turn over all evidence to the defense that might exonerate their client."

"That seems only fair," Millie agreed.

"It is, and violating the rule is a serious offense that can mean up to twenty years in a federal prison for the prosecutor."

Marsha flipped through her stack and pulled out a couple of pages, pushing up her glasses to scan through them. "I have half a dozen Brady violations here that Mitch was responsible for. Like, John Bennett, who was sent away for 25 years to life for murder. He was recently released on appeal when his attorney produced a date-and-time-marked videotape of Mr. Bennett at a hotel a hundred miles away at the time of the crime. I found a note about this video in the case file from ten years ago."

"When was he released?" Alex asked.

"Two weeks ago."

Alex's jaw dropped. "Oh, my God. He could be the one."

"Maybe, but there are other possibilities," the paralegal advised. "Here's another one — a Henry

Barstow — who was released a month ago after a federal appeals court cleared him of attempted murder charges, finding that Mr. Stuart had 'knowingly elicited false testimony in winning a conviction.' I added this to my file recently after the City of Mobile had to pay $2.3 million dollars in compensation to the victim. This case could also point to an outraged city official who would want to retaliate, as well."

"Wasn't Mr. Stuart held accountable for these bogus prosecutions?" Alex asked.

The paralegal shrugged. "He was given a reprimand by the State Attorney's office in this last case, which is how I became aware of it."

She picked up a second paper. "Here's another case where the prisoner was released when his attorney proved in an appeal that there had been exculpatory evidence withheld. Again, the City paid compensation, but Mr. Stuart was only reprimanded there, too. He claimed he had no knowledge that this evidence existed — that one of the Assistant D.A.'s must not have given him proper notice."

Millie cleared her throat. "So, we have several cases where Mitch intentionally withheld or tampered with evidence. Are there other ways he mishandled cases?"

"Well, there's the other side of prosecutorial misconduct. There were instances I heard about when Mr. Stuart had inexplicably dropped the charges against a defendant, or substantially reduced them to lower a sentence. I got some files out of storage and found cancelled checks that were made out to Mitch Stuart, personally. One has to think, why would defendants need to pay Mr. Stuart for his work on their cases?"

Alex crossed her arms and leaned back. "How many cases do you have like that?"

"Another three that I found." She held up some pages. "Yes, I have three here."

"Were there any young female defendants who unaccountably received favorable treatment?" Alex asked.

"Oh, you mean the 'too pretty for prison' ones. Sure. There are maybe ten who were charged with prostitution or drugs who Mitch let off."

Alex made a face. "I guess that's just par for the course around here. Do you have their names, too?"

The paralegal nodded. "I have a list of the most recent female defendants who got off. Of course, those cases are harder to prove as prosecutorial misconduct as they're subjective; unlike Brady violations which have factual bases."

"But the young women may be the more likely suspects," Alex suggested. "We had thought the manner of killing — poisoning — would likely be done by a woman as it doesn't require the physical strength to overpower a man."

"That's a good point," the paralegal responded. "I hadn't thought of that. I've been thinking the murderer was a man, since men are far more likely to kill than women — 85 percent of murders are committed by men. I'll make you a copy of the list of names and contact information I have for each category — Brady violations, the personal checks, and questionable lenience cases, and you can take it from there."

Alex and Millie gathered their belongings and prepared to stand. "Thanks, Ms. Grayson," Alex said. "We're grateful that you took us into your confidence to share all this information."

The paralegal pushed back her chair and closed her file. "Just don't tell anyone where you got this. For your sake, I hope your friend didn't murder Mr. Stuart; although, for my sake, I hope it isn't someone who's seeking vengeance on our department. It's a bad business all around."

Chapter 26

IT WAS GETTING ON to five o'clock when Alex and Millie pulled into Rosemary's driveway.

The doorbell was quickly answered by Dottie who looked tired but happy to see them. "Rosemary and Josie are just finishing up some things," she advised. "We were thinking we'd go to Cyril's as soon as you got here. We can compare notes there and you'd have time to talk to whoever you want."

"Good idea," Millie responded. "I think we could all use a glass of wine — and something to eat while we're at it."

Twenty minutes later, the five of them squeezed inside the bar and stood behind others who were looking for a place to sit. Like the time before, the air was filled with the bouncy beat of Latin-style music competing with the din of patrons celebrating the end of the workday. Strings of lights still hung above the bar for the Mardi Gras season.

After a few minutes, the five women had moved up to be first in line to find a table. The man Alex recognized as the owner, Cyril Green, approached them, smiling. "There are some tables in the back, ladies. Sit wherever you can find seats."

"Thanks," Alex said, then edged over close to him. "I don't know if you remember us," she said, in a low voice, "but we were here a couple nights ago with the District Attorney, Mitch Stuart. I think you know him?"

Green shrugged one shoulder. "I-I might recognize him . . . if I saw him," he conceded.

"I believe he was a regular here. I remember seeing you having a long conversation with him then so I thought you'd want to know that he was murdered last night."

Green stared at her. "Murdered?"

"Poisoned — at a Mardi Gras party. I'm sorry to just blurt out something like that, but there isn't any privacy here." She gestured at the crowd. "Mitch said he came here quite often, so I thought you'd want to know."

Green straightened and pulled at his shirt collar like it was suddenly too tight. "Uh, yes. Yes. He was a bit of a regular, now that I think about it. Thank you for telling me. I'm sure it's a terrible thing for his family and for the County of Mobile, considering he was the Chief Prosecuting Attorney."

Alex nodded. "His widow is here with us. We felt she needed to get out — y'know, to put all of this out of her mind for a little while."

Green glanced over at Rosemary. "I'm glad you did and that you came here. I'd like you all to have drinks and whatever you want to eat — on me."

Alex held up her hands in protest.

"No, I insist. I'll tell your waitress after you get seated. It's my pleasure. It's the least I can do to honor someone who worked so hard to keep our city safe."

Alex managed to keep her composure, then smiled and thanked him for his generosity on Rosemary's behalf. Turning to the others, she motioned for them to make their way toward the back.

The last unoccupied table for six was all the way in the rear of the restaurant, in proximity of the restrooms and the two doors that were designated for Employees Only.

After they were seated, Alex related her conversation with Cyril Green.

"That's odd, isn't it?" Josie mused, "that he denied even knowing Mitch at first, and then admitted he was a regular, and finally insisted on treating us to dinner. I mean, why the dodge?"

"That's what I'd like to know," Alex responded. "I tried to catch him off guard by bringing up Mitch's murder out of the blue — but I have to admit he seemed genuinely surprised."

"Alex sees everyone as the murderer until they can be eliminated," Millie cracked.

Alex snickered. "I think we've all felt there was something strange going on here. Mitch denied he frequented the place and yet, everyone here seemed to know him. And then there was what looked like an angry confrontation between Mitch and Cyril Green at the door. I tried to draw Green out about that conversation, but he didn't bite. He could have easily told me that Mitch was complaining about unruly kids outside if it was true, but he didn't. Anyway, that's why we're here — to uncover Mitch's secretive relationship with this place. It's a perfectly reputable bar, so why all the secrecy and denials?"

A twenty-something, blue-eyed, blond waitress approached their table and handed out menus. Alex caught Millie's eye to signal that this was the same waitress who whispered into Mitch's ear at the bar Monday night.

"Welcome, ladies," she said, tossing back her ponytail. "My name is Taylor and I'll be taking care of you. Mr. Green told me that he's treating all of you this evening. May I ask what's the special occasion?"

The women exchanged glances before Rosemary spoke up. "Uh, this is a little awkward. Mr. Cyril is generously honoring my husband who sadly . . . passed away last night."

The waitress blanched. "Oh, I'm so sorry! Mr. Green should have told me and I wouldn't have embarrassed y'all like this." She looked down and fingered her order pad.

"No need to apologize," Rosemary said. "We've been talking about nothing else, really."

"We understand that her husband, Mitch Stuart, was a regular here," Alex commented.

Taylor's eyes widened in shock. "Mitch Stuart?" she repeated, breathlessly. "He died?!"

"You must have known him from waiting on him many times," Millie suggested, baiting her.

Taylor's face had gone blank. "Uh, yes. Of course. Please excuse me. I need to pick up some plates from the kitchen. I'll be back to take your drink orders."

She turned and hurried toward the kitchen, dabbing at her face.

Rosemary picked up her napkin and smoothed it over her lap. "We seem to have upset the young lady. I wonder why?" She made a face. "I'm thinking Mitch's death will be upsetting pretty, young women all over Mobile. That reminds me, Dottie, why don't you tell everyone what you found out. Then, I can't wait to hear what happened at Mitch's office and the Public Defender's Office."

Dottie gave a little shrug. "I don't have all that much to report. I think Rosemary wants me to tell you that I found Stacy Gibson — if it's the same Stacy Gibson you saw at the parade. She's working as a housekeeper at the Candlewood Suites downtown. I told the desk clerk I'm a family friend visiting for Mardi Gras and I wanted to stop by to surprise her to say 'hello.' The clerk didn't hesitate to confirm that she works there and that she'll be at the hotel tomorrow."

"Nice work," Alex said.

"Yeah, I have to admit I'm a pretty good liar. I even thought to say it would be a surprise so she wouldn't tell Stacy."

Alex smiled. "I'll go see her tomorrow morning. I'm not sure what to ask her, except how well she knew Mitch, and if she knew of other women he was seeing—whatever I can think of. It depends on what she says, what I'll ask. Did you get a list of the current inmates in Alabama?"

"You think I'd be here if I didn't? As you suggested, I Googled the Alabama Department of Corrections and clicked on current incarcerations and printed it out. Do you want the bad news?"

Alex wrinkled her nose. "Don't tell me — there weren't any matches with our guest list."

Dottie pointed at her. "Right. There were a few matches of common surnames, but nothing jumped out like, say, a Hickenlooper or a Dumbledore that had a match. I showed Rosemary the list to see if she recognized any names that maybe were related to Goddesses, but she didn't know any of them."

The women looked up as Taylor returned with her mascara smeared around her reddened eyes. "I'm sorry to have kept you waiting. Do you know what you'd like to drink? And if you're ready to order your dinner, I can take care of that, too."

They went around the table, quickly scanning the page of the menu that listed entrees and made their selections and ordered wine.

"Thanks. I'll be right back with your drinks," Taylor said, quietly, then turned and left.

Rosemary rolled her eyes. "Mitch must have been helping her with her rent. This is getting sickening. First, there's that call girl, Stacy Gibson, and now this girl who has a ponytail, for God's sake."

Alex covered her smile. "Not to change the subject . . . but, since there's only one subject — what did you and Josie find when you compared the names of people in the D.A.'s office with the guest list?"

Just then Taylor returned. The women remained silent as the young woman set down a glass of wine at each of their places. As she left, Rosemary stuck out her tongue at her back, and then answered Alex. "Like Dottie said, we found people with two or three of the same surnames, but they're common in the South, like Williams and Brown. We didn't find any full names that matched anyone on the guest list. Almost all the women in the Goddesses are married. Without knowing their own family names, I wouldn't recognize any connections."

"There were ten names that were added by hand who weren't invited guests," Josie said. "Maybe the police could check them out."

Rosemary looked over at Alex. "What did you and Millie find out at the Public Defender's and Mitch's office?"

Alex glanced at Millie who nodded once for her to answer. "Well, we heard a lot about how Mitch discharged his duties as Chief Prosecutor and none of it was very positive. Both Jenkins, the Public Defender, and Mitch's paralegal described Mitch's actions as totally corrupt."

Rosemary covered her face with her hands. "Really?" she asked in a small voice.

"I'm sorry, but to put it in cop's parlance, Mitch was dirty. He took bribes, he withheld exculpatory evidence, and he was lenient on young women, possibly in exchange for sexual favors. The point is, Rosemary, he wasn't just dishonest with you. He was dishonest with the 200,000 people who live in Mobile County. From what we heard, he was probably a State Attorney's referral away from losing his law license and being sent away to Federal prison. Millie and I got the names of about twenty people who were either unjustly convicted or mysteriously had their charges dropped."

Rosemary hung her head and sobbed softly into her napkin.

Alex clasped her hands in front of her. "I'm sorry to tell you all this, but you had to know the truth. In time, it will be better that you know. And I believe one of these names will lead us to his killer. Whatever Mitch did as a man and as a public official, he still didn't deserve to be poisoned like a rat in the barn."

Rosemary looked up, brushing away her tears. "Listen, I don't want you to talk to any convicts who served time just to help me. Like you say, it's possible one of them is a murderer. And we can't investigate twenty people in one day, anyway. You need to turn over all those names to Detective Langford to investigate. Promise me you'll do that."

Alex twisted her mouth in thought. "I'll promise you that I won't talk to the men who served time, however unjustly, but I'd like to try to track down the women who were let off on non-violent charges. I believe it's more likely the murderer was a woman, but I'll only go as far as to see who had alibis for the time of the party, and can be eliminated."

Taylor reappeared with their dinners, still looking shaken.

Rosemary rolled her eyes. "I think she's taking Mitch's murder harder than I am," she said sourly after the young woman left.

"You're being a real trooper," Josie said. "Mitch didn't deserve you."

"Let's just enjoy our dinner," Dottie proposed with an upbeat tone.—,"and let's drink to better days," she added, raising her glass.

Rosemary barely lifted hers, but managed to take a sip. "I'd say the days can only get better after this."

While they ate, the conversation turned to the latest ghostly activities at the Granada Inn. Josie reported on finding the two lamps that had been unplugged when she got back to the room last night after the party. Both she and Alex were certain they had been plugged in when they went up to the room during the party. Dottie wondered if the ghosts were trying to scare them away. If so, they were doing a good job of it. Alex wondered if there had been human intervention to make it look like there were ghosts. Everyone agreed that it was disturbing to find the lamps being tampered with by whoever or whatever when the rooms were locked.

As they were finishing their cheeseburgers and chicken baskets, Alex's attention was drawn to something over Rosemary's right shoulder. "Has anyone else noticed the men in business suits going through that door marked Employees Only?"

Millie lifted her chin in thought. "You know, I was thinking they were going into the men's room, but you're right — that's the next one over."

Alex tossed her napkin down next to her plate. "I want to see what's behind that door."

Josie grabbed her arm. "Hold on. You don't know what you're getting into. I see a busboy over there. Why don't you just ask him? It could be some private men's club meeting in there and you'll just embarrass yourself."

Alex pushed back her chair and stood for a moment, uncertain which way to go, then headed over to the Employees Only door. Turning around, she pantomimed to her friends that she was just going to take a peek.

The four women looked intently as she cracked open the door and stood listening for a moment, and then disappeared inside.

Millie rose from her chair. "I think I'd better go after her. She has no fear, that woman."

Just as Millie approached the door, Alex emerged and took Millie by the arm to walk back to rejoin the others at the table.

"Well?" Rosemary asked as Alex sat down. "What's in there?"

Alex leaned back sat and folded her arms, looking smug. "Would you believe — a gambling casino?"

"You mean, like a professional set-up, or just a table with a few guys playing poker? Millie asked.

"I mean, the whole kit and caboodle — roulette, craps, poker, and a couple slot machines thrown in for good measure."

"Wow, who would have thought all that would be behind that innocent little door in the back of a bar?" Josie asked, rhetorically.

"Did they notice you walking in on them?" Dottie asked.

"They glanced over at me, but they were too engrossed in their games to react. I suppose they let women in at times, but there were only men now."

"I wonder why the door doesn't say 'Casino' instead of 'Employees Only'?" Dottie asked with a smirk.

Alex snorted a laugh. "Yeah, I wonder. Maybe, because gambling is illegal in Alabama. And, maybe, because Cyril Green would lose his liquor license if the state licensing board became aware of this. I think we know now why Mitch denied that he came around here much — besides his girlfriend. I think it's a safe bet, pun intended, that Cyril Green was paying hush money to Mitch to run this illegal gambling operation. And I bet *the house* that Cyril Green has a felony record and illegally holds a liquor license in the first place, so he might as well go for broke since he had the highest law enforcement official in the county in his pocket."

"Holy crap," Rosemary muttered. "I think this explains one of the regular monthly deposits I found in Mitch's checkbook. I wonder what else we'll find out."

Alex held up her hands. "I don't know, but I can't wait until tomorrow. I think we're getting close to naming Mitch's murderer."

Chapter 27

THE NEXT MORNING, Alex pushed open the glass door into the Candlewood Suites hotel, still wondering what she was going to ask Stacy Gibson that could lead to Mitch's killer. She still believed that a woman was most likely the perpetrator, so every female relationship had to be thoroughly explored. This was the last full day the four of them would be in Mobile to help Rosemary follow-up on the leads they had regarding Mitch's activities and involvements.

They had all agreed to the assignments she had given them when they met for breakfast: Rosemary would give Detective Langford the names of the men Mitch had unjustly convicted by withholding evidence. Dottie and Millie would meet with the president of the Goddesses to see if she knew if any of the names on the Public Defender's and District Attorney's lists had any connections with her group. Josie would finish looking through Mitch's desk, his files, and emails and any other social media on his computer.

Inside the Candlewood lobby, Alex approached the young female desk clerk, flashing a smile. "Good morning. I called yesterday to check if Stacy Gibson was still a housekeeper here."

The woman nodded. "Yes, I remember. "You're related to her."

"Right. A distant relative. I'm just on my way out of town so I won't take but a few minutes of her time."

"Sure, that's fine," the clerk said, then checked her watch. "She'll still be up on the top floor. The elevator's right over there."

Alex breathed a sigh of relief as she boarded the empty elevator and pushed '3.' So far, so good, she thought. Hopefully, Stacy would be willing to talk to her and would have some useful information.

Getting out of the car, she headed down the hallway toward a housekeeping cart with supplies and peeked into the nearby open door. The slim redhead pulling sheets off one of the double beds looked younger without the heavy makeup she had been wearing when Alex had seen her at the parade.

"Stacy?" Alex said, coming into the room.

The housekeeper jerked in surprise. "Yes, ma'am, I'm Stacy. Did you need some towels or somethin'?"

"No, I just wanted to talk to you for a minute. My name is Alex Trotter. I'm a friend of Rosemary

Stuart's. I wanted to ask you a little about Mitch Stuart."

Stacy took a step back, losing her smile.

"Uh, Mitch told Rosemary that he helped you out and —"

Stacy raised one hand like a traffic cop. "I don't want no trouble. I work hard and take care of myself. I been off the streets for six months."

"That's great. I'm not here to cause any problems for you. Like I said, I know you were a friend of Mitch's, but I don't know if you've heard he died Tuesday night."

Stacy blanched and dropped onto the bed. "Mitch died?"

"Actually, he was murdered at a Mardi Gras party. Poisoned. His wife has been questioned as a suspect, but I know she didn't do it. I wondered if you might know of anyone who would want to see him dead. Did you know any other women he 'helped out'?

Stacy pressed her fingers into her temples. "I thought he was a good man. Maybe some others didn't like the arrangements he made to keep them out of prison."

Alex sat on the other bed across from the housekeeper. "You mean . . . sexual favors?" she asked in a low voice.

Stacy shrugged. "It was better than hustling for johns who would knock you around."

"I'm sure," Alex agreed. "Did you know any women who didn't like the 'arrangements,' as you called them?"

"I dunno. I don't wanna squeal on anyone. I know there were some who didn't usually turn tricks who might have thought the arrangement was a big deal. I met a few of them when I got picked up in a sting operation. Four of us were held in one cell overnight. I got to talkin' to the other three. They wasn't regulars on the street. I think they was just out cuz they needed money for drugs."

Alex held her breath. "Maybe, just give me the names of those three who weren't working girls. I promise I won't get them in trouble by giving their names to the police."

Stacy twisted her mouth, staring off into space. "All right, if it don't go no further than you. Let's see. There was Candice Brown, and Carlotta Dorado, and Deanna Adams. Nice girls. Just got into the drug scene. After we got out, I'd see them on the street now and then, but I haven't seen them for a while. I know they took the deal from Mitch, but I don't think they liked it. They were all very young and pretty so I think that's why they were offered the arrangement."

Alex pulled a small notebook out of her purse and wrote in it. "Thanks, Stacy. I appreciate your confiding in me. I'm sorry I had to be the one to tell you about Mitch being murdered."

Stacy blinked back tears and waved away the comment. "That's okay. I just hope those young girls didn't have nothin' to do with the murder — or Mrs. Stuart, neither. I can't imagine who would do such a terrible thing to Mitch. He was a nice guy."

After her visit with Stacy Gibson, Alex drove back to the Granada Inn to wait for Dottie and Millie to return with the list of women whose cases had been dismissed by Mitch. Feeling hungry and needing to while away some time, she parked her car and headed over to the Carriage House.

The place was empty except for one couple seated at the end of the bar. Alex thought the lack of business was probably due to Mardi Gras being over and that many people gave up drinking alcoholic beverages for lent.

She took a stool at the other end from the other two patrons. The bartender soon sauntered over and handed her a menu, then ran a damp cloth over the glossy wood surface in front of her. Alex noticed his name tag read 'Chad'. He was a pleasant-looking young man with sandy-colored hair and brown eyes. She skimmed down the menu and decided on a shrimp salad and a glass of Chablis.

"Thanks," he said. "I'll get your wine and the salad should be right up."

After handing the order to the kitchen, he brought her wine over and set it down in front of her. Leaning back against the liquor case, he smiled at her. "Have your friends left?" he asked.

She blinked. "Oh . . . no. They're just out for a little while. This is our last day here so we've split up to do different things. I'm, uh, surprised you noticed our group."

"Well, there are mostly couples here, especially for Mardi Gras, so five attractive women stand out — even more than usual." He smiled more broadly and crossed his arms over his chest.

Alex could see that he wanted to stay and chat as there wasn't much business. Maybe he had seen something Tuesday night he wanted to talk about. "Thanks for the compliment. It was our friend's husband, the County District Attorney, who was murdered here Tuesday night."

"Yeah, I heard. I'm sorry for your friend. Do the police have any leads on who poisoned the guy?"

"Not really. Actually, my friends and I have been digging around, trying to come up with some suspects. We got a list of people Mr. Stuart convicted who may have carried a grudge, but we haven't been able to make any connections with people who were here for the party."

Chad shifted crossed his legs. "Maybe you should investigate like the police do and look at people close to the victim."

"Rosemary's been questioned, but I was with her when Stuart was poisoned, so it couldn't have been her. We don't know anyone he was close to who was here Tuesday night."

Chad scratched his chin and gazed up at the ceiling. "I was thinking, by 'close,' maybe someone who works here. I mean, the guy got his drink out there in the courtyard. Who made his drink, or who was right there when he got it? I was tending bar out here for a while."

Alex gave him an impish look. "Are you confessing?"

Chad slapped the bar cloth on his leg. "Hell, I didn't even know the guy. I'd only kill someone I know."

They both looked in the direction of the kitchen as his name was called.

"That must be your shrimp salad. I'll be right back."

Setting it down moments later he said, "I'll let you enjoy your meal. Some people just came in so I need to go, anyway."

Alex mixed the dressing around with her fork. "Well, thanks for the talk. You've given me some ideas. I hadn't really thought about the staff here at the Inn."

"Yeah, well don't tell anyone I squealed on them," he said, grinning.

Alex nodded and smiled back. "That's what everyone says who gives me information."

Chapter 28

ALEX FINISHED HER SALAD, paid the bill in cash, and left a generous tip for Chad. *One good tip deserves another*, she said to herself as she swung off the bar stool and headed towards the door.

Crossing the courtyard, her mind went back to Tuesday night. Betsy was the first one on the scene. What did they really know about the woman? The name Betsy was probably a nickname for Elizabeth, so she wouldn't have recognized her name if it had been on one of the lists from the prosecutor's office. What was her last name again?—oh, yeah, Davis. That sounded like an alias. Her name could be Elizabeth Davis and she wouldn't have given it a second thought.

At the back of the Inn, she pushed open the door and walked into the lobby. Betsy now looked suspicious as she sat behind the front desk in her usual place. Alex waved at the manager in greeting.

Betsy looked up and smiled. *Or was that a smirk?* "Hi, Miss Alex. Your friends just came back — Miss

Millie and Miss Dottie. Nice young ladies. Always stop and chat a bit."

Alex rested her crossed arms on the reception counter. "They probably want to get to know you a little better. We went through that tragic murder Tuesday night with you and we don't know much about you. Like, were you born in Mobile?"

"I think you can hear that in my accent. Yes, I sure was. My daddy was minister of the First Baptist Church and my mother was the organist and even directed the choir. Daddy always joked that it would have been cheaper to have hired a music director and have stayed single as Mama enjoyed buyin' little trinkets for herself and the three of us girls. That was her biggest sin," she added, chuckling.

Alex felt her shoulders sag in disappointment. "How did you get into this business?" she asked, rebounding a little.

Betsy looked away. "Well, after high school, I took classes in hospitality management at USA — er, the University of South Alabama — I think because Mama always had church people over to the house, and I found I enjoyed that — entertaining people and making them feel at home. I was thinking I would get a job at a resort up in the mountains or on the coast, but both Daddy and Mama had health problems early on, so I became their caretaker for several years and needed to work here in Mobile. As a child I had always loved the look of this place even back when it was two houses, so when this job became available years ago, I took it. I've been here so long it's easy for me to think of this place as my own home."

Alex slumped more heavily on the counter. "You never married?"

Betsy sighed. "No. what with caring for my parents and working here, I never had much of a social life with a lot of dating. I don't meet many single men at this old inn, as you can imagine, so I've been content to think of my staff as my family."

Alex felt her head pitching forward and righted herself. "I never asked on Tuesday night, but did you know Mitch Stuart before the party?"

"I knew the name because he was the County District Attorney, and I think I voted for him, but I don't believe I ever met him. And, of course, in that disguise, I wouldn't have recognized him if I had. That's a terrible way to learn who a person is, isn't it? — reaching into his bag for his I.D. when he's dying?" She blinked back tears and shook her head as though to clear away the thought.

Alex lowered her eyes and nodded to imitate Betsy's show of respect. "You did all you could do to help him," she said softly. "I'm sure the staff felt terrible that you had to be responsible in that situation. I noticed they kept on working, so that most of the guests never realized there had been a murder."

Betsy's face cleared. "You're so right. They were all troopers, carrying on as though nothing had happened. I'm sure they didn't want to ruin the party for everyone."

"Have they all worked here for a long time?" Alex asked, trying to make it sound like casual conversation.

"Well, some of the girls—Lupe, Sofie, and Linda haven't been here that long, but they're all good girls and good workers. The two I depend on the most—Diego Herrera, my head porter and all-around right-hand man, and Maria Dorado, my head housekeeper—have been here a long time. Over five years."

Alex stood up straight, feeling the blood leave her face. "Dorado is kind of an unusual name, isn't it?"

Betsy shrugged. "I guess. I haven't heard the name except for Maria. It means 'land of riches.' I think Maria thinks of Mobile as a sort of paradise. She's so grateful for her life here. Actually, she's leaving today for a week. I think she's going back to Mexico to be with her family there, after what she's been through. I told you about her daughter."

Alex swallowed to relieve her dry mouth. "Yes, you did; right after I arrived. That reminds me, do you think she could take me down to the tunnel yet today? Dottie and I explored it with Diego but I had forgotten my cell phone so I didn't get any pictures. I've been thinking Mobile is an ideal location for my professional groups to have their conferences and I know they'd all love to stay at the Granada. I'd like to get some shots of the tunnel since it's such a unique feature. I've taken pictures of our guest rooms and the lobby of course."

Betsy's eyes shone with the prospect of multiple bookings. "I'm sure she'd have a few minutes." She checked her watch. "It's a little after two, and she leaves at four o'clock, so I think there's time."

"Great. I need to change first, anyway. Could you ask her to meet me at the door to the tunnel at say, three o'clock?"

"That should be fine. If there's any problem, I'll call up to your room."

"Thanks so much, Betsy. That'll be a big help to me."

Alex felt she couldn't get upstairs fast enough. Hurrying out of the lobby and into the west townhouse, she rushed down the hall to the staircase. Grabbing the newel post, she propelled herself up the stairs to the second floor. At the top, she quickly walked down the hallway to Room 206 and knocked on the door.

Millie opened it, then jumped back as Alex burst in. "Sorry to rush in like this but I couldn't wait to tell you my news. You didn't find out anything from that Goddess lady, did you?" she asked, glancing between Dottie and Millie.

"No. What are you — psychic?" Millie asked with a smirk.

"Not exactly, although I now know who the murderer is."

Dottie dropped the book she was reading in a chair in the opposite corner. "What?!"

Millie led Alex over to another chair. "Okay, sit down and start at the beginning to tell us what you've come up with and why you think you can name the killer."

"Not think. Know."

"Right. You now *know* who the killer is," Millie corrected herself. "Wait — you went to see that redheaded woman, Stacy Gibson, this morning. Is she the killer?"

"No, but she gave me my most important clue. After seeing her, I came back to the hotel and stopped at the Carriage House for a bite to eat and talked to Chad the bartender."

"Chad the bartender is the killer," Dottie announced breathlessly.

"No, of course not; but I was talking to him about how we're going all over town looking for suspects, and he said maybe we're going too far afield and we should be looking closer to home."

Millie and Dottie raised their eyebrows, waiting to hear more.

"Anyway, it got me thinking that we've only tried to find connections to people at the party with outsiders; fixating on who could have a motive. Chad was saying, why didn't we start with the people who were here, physically close to Mitch when he was poisoned?"

Millie folded her arms. "Go on," she said, doubtfully.

"I'm still thinking it was Chad," Dottie chimed in. "He wanted to get Mitch out of the way so he could have Rosemary to himself," she declared, grinning.

Alex rolled her eyes. "I'm being serious, here," she reminded them. "Where was I? Oh, yes, so I thought I'd follow up on Chad's advice and look into people who work here at the hotel, and I thought right away that we don't know much about Betsy."

Millie sat bolt upright, "so, Betsy's the killer?"

Alex put her head down for several moments, before looking up again. "No— but I thought about that possibility until I talked to her. Turns out she's like the 'Mother Maria of Mobile.' She's been taking care of people since she was a kid. Her life story just about made me sick. But she did inadvertently supply the solution to the mystery. A solution that had been in my subconscious, but hadn't come to the surface yet."

"Are you going to ever tell us who the killer was?" Millie asked, pretending to yawn.

"You people are terrible," Alex countered. "If you'll indulge me, let me remind you of a couple of things we kept coming back to: Mitch was disguised in his costume as Richard the Lion Hearted—"

"Braveheart," Millie and Dottie said in unison.

Alex chuckled. "I know—just seeing if you were paying attention. Anyway, we kept saying that no one could have recognized him if they didn't know his costume beforehand."

"But there was no way we could know who he might have told," Dottie contended.

"Right — but stay with me here. Mitch wore a kilt with the costume. He was the only man at the party in a kilt, so one just had to know about the kilt to be able to recognize him."

Millie and Dottie looked blankly at her.

Alex waved aside the skepticism to continue. "So, we knew that he could have been positively identified by his kilt. Another factor was that we felt it was a woman who killed him because poison didn't require strength. Thirdly, we could assume there had to be a strong motive to kill him in front of a couple hundred people, risking being caught in the act. It was improbable that Mitch was killed by some stranger who was a psychopath who had wandered in. It had to be someone who appeared to be normal. Now, here's where we come to what I had in the back of my mind."

Millie turned to Dottie. "Hold on to your hat."

Alex shook her head. "Listen, carefully. When I arrived at the hotel last Sunday, I was the first guest to check in so Betsy had time to show me around and tell me about the ghosts and all. She asked Maria, the head housekeeper, to watch the desk for a few minutes while we went outside. In our conversation she mentioned that Maria was sullen because her daughter Carlotta had just died and the girl was all she had. Betsy said Carlotta was a beautiful, bright girl but had gotten in with the wrong crowd and was using drugs. The cause of her death was undetermined, but probably was an overdose. So, anyway, that was that."

"Okay, got it," Millie said, circling her finger in the air for Alex to move on with her story.

"So, soon after that, Rosemary stopped by and we sat in that small lounge to visit before you both came. You know where I mean—where we ate during the party and where Detective Langford questioned us."

"We know, we know," Millie said, impatiently.

Alex raised her hands. "Anyway, Rosemary and I talked a little about her marital problems, but said they also had good times, and he was looking forward to meeting us, hopefully before the party. I distinctly remember her telling me that Mitch was dressing up as Robert the Bruce, who was Braveheart, because *he wanted to wear a kilt.*"

"Oh, my goodness," Millie said in mock horror.

Alex leaned forward in her chair. "I also remember that Maria had just then entered the sitting room to dust the furniture. That's what I had tucked away in my subconscious mind whenever we brought up the fact that Mitch was totally disguised by his costume."

"I don't think that's enough to get a conviction, Millie said, dryly.

"Hear me out. Then we all got onto the fact that Mitch was likely trading sex for dropping charges against certain young women, and we got some names from Mitch's paralegal that you two went over with that Goddess woman. Meanwhile, Rosemary met with Detective Langford to give him the names of the men who were unjustly convicted.

"I didn't look at the names on either of those lists. But this morning, when I met with Stacy Gibson — who is very nice, by the way, and seemed to care about Mitch — she 9999gave me the names of three young girls who were drug users who were caught up in a prostitution sweep with her and were kept in the same cell overnight with her.

"She told me that before their trials, those three girls agreed to Mitch's 'arrangement,' as she called it, which was to exchange sex for their freedom. One of the young girls was Carlotta Delgado." She looked at Dottie and Millie who didn't react. "When I just talked to Betsy, she mentioned that Maria's name is Maria Delgado. That's not a common name. *Maria is Carlotta's mother.* I'm certain that Maria knew Carlotta was being used by Mitch Stuart and believed that he was responsible for her death — either by supporting her habit so that she overdosed, or intentionally giving her an overdose if she threatened to rat him out to the State Attorney.

"Maria is the only person who had the knowledge, the motive, and the opportunity to kill Mitch, and could get away with it. She was serving drinks so she had easy access to Mitch's drink. She wouldn't have been noticed being around at the time he was poisoned, because a waitress is invisible. How often do you forget what your waitress looks like? She knew who Rosemary was from her visit, and saw the costume Rosemary brought to the inn to change into. It would have been easy for Maria to slip the poison bottle into her pocket, too.

"Lastly, think about the lamps being unplugged in our rooms. Maria has a passkey, and had reason to want us to leave. She overheard us talking about investigating the murder, so she took advantage of the rumors of ghosts unplugging lamps. But what will positively identify her as the killer is if her fingerprint is on the poison bottle. There's no innocent explanation for her print to be there."

Millie collapsed against the back of her chair. "Wow. I shouldn't have teased you. That's absolutely brilliant."

"It all makes perfect sense," Dottie agreed. "I'll bet her print is on that bottle and that's all Detective Langford will need to arrest her and hold her for trial."

Millie sat forward. "So, what now?"

"Well, that's where you come in. Betsy said Maria's leaving for Mexico today. She thinks it's for a vacation because of her grief over losing Carlotta. I think she's going on the lam to never be heard from again. I had to come up with a way to be sure she doesn't leave before Langford can arrest her so I arranged with Betsy to have Maria take me down to the tunnel, telling her that I didn't have my phone to take pictures last time. I'm supposed to meet Maria at three o'clock by the hallway door. I want you to call Detective Langford and tell him all that I've told you so he'll come right over to arrest her."

Millie's jaw dropped. "Are you crazy? You can't go into the tunnel with that murderess."

"She *poisoned* Mitch. I don't think she can poison me in the tunnel. Besides, she doesn't know I figured out that she murdered him. I have to go change now to meet her, but here's Detective Langford's card so you can reach him directly. Be sure he understands we know that Maria's the killer."

"I don't know," Millie said, wincing.

"Look, I'll have my phone and I've got your number in my contacts. If anything goes wrong, I'll call you, but Langford should be here before I'm even out of the tunnel. I'm sure this case is a priority for him so he won't be too busy to respond. He met with Rosemary earlier so he's probably back at the station." She got up from her chair and went to the door. "I'm going now to change and meet with Maria, so . . . good luck."

Millie stood to see her out. "I think you're the one who needs the luck. All right, I'll call Langford. Hope to see you alive and well in about half an hour."

Chapter 29

ALEX CAUTIOUSLY PADDED down the stairs at five minutes to three, feeling her heart pounding in her chest. Rounding the corner, she saw Maria standing by the hallway door to the tunnel, her hands buried in her pockets.

"Hi, Maria."

The housekeeper nodded once.

"Hey, I'm sorry to trouble you with this, but it shouldn't take more than a few minutes."

Maria made a point of looking at her watch. "I don't have much time, *Señora*." She turned the knob of the hallway door, pushed it open, and stood back for Alex to enter the cramped room.

"Here, I'll pull up the cover," Alex said, leaning over to lift off the plywood square. "Do you have a flashlight? Otherwise, I have one on my phone."

Maria reached into her pocket and pulled out a penlight.

Alex looked at it dubiously. "That . . . might be okay for our purposes. I'll be taking pictures with a flash, anyway." She looked down the hole. "Uh, do you want me to go first?"

"*Si*. You go. Then I'll go."

"Okay, just shine the light for me." Alex got down on her knees and backed up to the opening. Extending one leg, she felt for a step on the ladder with her foot. Finding one, she pushed her other leg through the hole and half-stepped and half-slid down the smooth ladder. "I'm on the ground," she called up.

Maria followed, keeping the flashlight in front of herself, leaving Alex in the dark. "Where do you want to go?" Maria asked after she landed.

Like there's more than one way to go? Alex thought. "I'd like to go down as far as where the tunnel opens up higher." She held her hands up to the ceiling to make the point. "But, first, I want to take a picture of that little room where the soldiers camped out."

Without speaking, Maria started forward in a crouched position, keeping the small flashlight beam in front of her. Alex stayed close on the woman's heels to catch a glimpse of the opening ahead to keep her bearing. It was becoming obvious that Maria resented doing this and had no intention in trying to accommodate her. As they moved further into the tunnel, Alex started thinking this excursion was a bad idea. On the other hand, she didn't feel she was in any danger, so she could tolerate the housekeepers' rudeness for the next several minutes. After all, when they came out of the tunnel, she would be free to go on about her day and

Maria would be placed in handcuffs and taken away to a jail cell. The thought gave her renewed energy and tolerance to plow on ahead in the near-darkness.

"I think I see that recess ahead where the little cot is," Alex called out.

Maria grunted in response.

Moments later they reached the alcove. In the faint light, the army cot appeared to have disintegrated even further since the last time she was there. "Let's stop here and I'll take a few pictures." She pulled her cell phone out of her shirt pocket and pressed on the side button to turn it on. It stayed dark. She hit the Home button on the bottom of the screen. Still nothing. She tried every button before she realized her battery must be too low or she couldn't get a signal in a tunnel. Why hadn't she checked that? She couldn't let Maria know because she'd insist on leaving immediately. She'd have to fake it.

"Maria, could you shine the light on the army cot and the room? My camera flash isn't working."

The housekeeper turned the penlight to illuminate the scene while Alex pretended to shoot closeups of the cot and the blankets, then stood back to take the room itself. She slid the phone back into her pocket. "Okay, that should do it. Thanks."

Maria grunted again and took off deeper into the tunnel with Alex following. They continued on for several minutes until Alex became aware of the air becoming lighter and less dank. Over Maria's backside she saw that they had come to the opening to the higher chamber. "This is it, Maria. Let's stop and I'll take a few pictures and then we can go back."

Going through the opening, both women could stand up and stretch. "This is much better, isn't it?" Alex asked.

"*Si*. Better," Maria agreed, grudgingly.

Alex walked around a little in the more open space and took a few pictures in the semi-darkness before returning to the entrance where Maria had waited. "Okay, that should do it."

"We done now?" Maria asked.

"Yes, that's fine. I hope I haven't kept you too long. Betsy told me you're leaving for vacation today."

Maria glowered at her. "Si. I'm going home to see *mi familia*."

"That's good. I, uh, understand that you lost your daughter recently. I'm so sorry."

Maria's eyes narrowed. "I didn't *lose* her. She died at the hands of another. She was all I had and she was taken from me."

"She was murdered?"

Maria's dark eyes flashed. "Not with a knife or a gun, but it was murder just the same. That *cabron* took control of her and ruined her life. Then he killed her with drugs. I made sure he found out what it was like to die from drugs." Maria's face cleared as she turned to stare at Alex. "How did *you* hear about my Carlotta?"

"I, uh, didn't hear much about it. Betsy mentioned it; that she felt so bad for you." Maria swung the flashlight around to aim it at Alex's eyes blinding her. Alex felt her heart in her mouth.

After several seconds, Maria slowly dropped the beam down to her watch. "It's three thirty. I'm being picked up at four. I can't miss my ride."

Alex nodded, swallowing hard. "We can go quickly. You start and I'll keep up with you."

Maria ducked through the archway and stayed in a stooped position to start back while Alex followed, close behind.

After several minutes they reached the alcove with the soldier's bed, and five minutes later they were at the ladder. Maria shone the light into Alex's eyes again and pointed an accusing finger. "You were a friend of his," she spat out.

Alex blinked at the bright light, deciding not to play dumb. "No. I'm a friend of his wife's. I only met him twice. I didn't know anything about him."

Maria's face darkened. "I think you did. You've been snooping around and asking too many questions . . . and now you know too much. I'm sorry, but you have to stay here." She drew a pair of shears out of her pocket and held the scissors above her shoulder like a dagger. "Don't move. I don't want to hurt you. Your friends will come for you soon enough."

Maria quickly mounted the ladder and pulled it up behind her.

Alex called after her, "You're not getting away with this. I'm calling my friend who's waiting to hear from me."

"Har!" Maria sneered. "I saw your phone didn't work in the tunnel."

Alex held her cell directly under the hole and tapped hard on the side button. The apps came to life and she hit the phone icon, then contacts. "Millie! Maria's holding me in the tunnel. Get help. She's got long scissors."

Maria shone the light down the hole. "I don't think she could hear you without a connection. By the way, you can tell your detective friend that I killed Mitch Stuart, because I'll be long gone by the time you see him."

Suddenly, they heard thumping sounds coming from above, getting louder as they seemed to get closer to the closet. Maria turned toward the door just as it was banged open and Millie hurtled inside swinging Rosemary's scepter, knocking the scissors out of Maria's hand.

"*Ay! Ay! Ay!*" Maria screamed, covering her face with her hands as Millie kept striking her with the scepter. "*Vete al demonio, tarados*!"

Moments later, Dottie rushed in and grabbed Maria around the middle, pinning her arms to her sides. "I've got her!"

"*Mierda*!" Maria screamed, hurling spittle at both of them.

Running footsteps were heard out in the hallway. All three of them looked over to see

Detective Langford in the doorway. "All right, ladies. I think I better take over now before somebody gets hurt." He turned to Millie. "You got a license for that scepter?"

Langford took the handcuffs off his belt and snapped them on Maria's wrists behind her back.

"*Que te jodan!* she hissed at him.

"It's a good thing I don't know what that means, lady, or you could be in even more trouble than you already are."

"Hey guys, I'm down here!" Alex called out.

Langford looked over at Dottie and angled his head toward the ladder. "Would you mind? I've got my hands full here."

Dottie and Millie both lifted the ladder and slid it down the hole. Alex emerged from below just as Detective Langford was pushing his prisoner out the door. "I'll talk to you ladies later," he called back over his shoulder.

Alex gaped at her two friends, then embraced them. "Oh, brother! I don't think 'thank you' covers it. Would you both like to go to the Carriage House for a glass of wine — on me? I think we could use a little refreshment and maybe talk over some things."

Chapter 30

"I WISH YOU COULD'VE been there," Alex told Rosemary and Josie, wiping away tears from laughing so hard. "I was down below, but I could see Millie when she bulled her way through the doorway and smashed the scissors out of Maria's hand with that scepter. After Millie had walloped her a few more times I almost felt sorry for Maria. It reminded me of when we were in Terrace House and Millie chased that pervert Lawson down the stairs and thrashed him mercilessly with an umbrella until the police showed up."

"She's small, but she's a terror with an accessory that has a pointed end," Dottie joked, provoking more laughter.

The five of them were having dinner at Rosemary's on Thursday evening, reliving the events of the week and all they had learned about the murder. Alex had just brought Rosemary and Josie up to date on how she came upon the clues that led her to the discovery of the murderer, ending her narration with the story of her visit to the tunnel with Maria, Millie's heroic rescue, and Detective's Langford's timely arrival on the scene to arrest the housekeeper.

"I can see why you had to go down to the station to make a statement," Rosemary said after hearing how Alex had been involved with unraveling the mystery

Alex shrugged. "Detective Langford said he wanted all the details for the record, especially when the fingerprint on the aspirin bottle matched Maria's. He said we were way ahead of him; that he was still looking at the guest list. When I left the station, he joked that he'd call us to work the next murder."

Rosemary shook her head at the amazing development of her husband's murder being solved by her college friends. "Drew told me at lunch how impressed he was that we had investigated Mitch's conduct as county District Attorney."

"*Drew*?" Dottie asked.

Rosemary shrugged. "We arranged to meet for lunch for me to give him the names of the men who were unjustly convicted. Then we got to talking about a lot of different things." Her eyes glowed with interest. "He's really a nice guy. Easygoing — and funny, too, which was a welcome change from the many tense times I'd had with Mitch of late. Drew told me that he had hoped I wasn't the murderer because he was attracted to me."

Alex perked up. "Arlie told me the same thing when I was a murder suspect on Bedford Island!"

Millie made a groaning sound. "I think I'd prefer meeting someone when I'm *not* their murder suspect."

Ignoring Millie's comment, Alex asked Rosemary, "Are you going to see *Drew* again? I mean, after his investigation is concluded?"

"I know it's so soon after Mitch—uh, died— but I have a date with him Saturday night. He's taking me to a steakhouse in Fairhope on the other side of the bay. He thought it would be a nice change from seafood and give us a little excursion."

The others made silly cooing sounds in response.

Rosemary held up her hands. "No, I'm going to take this slow. The coroner is releasing Mitch's body today so I'm planning the funeral for Monday. I really don't want to think much beyond that right now. It'll take me a while to get over how he died, even though he was dishonest and hurt a lot of people."

"You're not thinking of moving back to New Jersey, are you?" Josie asked.

"No, my life is settled here. I love my job and I have friends here; but I will be putting the house on the market. In fact, I'm meeting with a real estate agent on Tuesday. Besides needing the money, I want to sell it because this was Mitch's house that I never felt was really mine. To tell you the truth, I always wondered how he could afford it on a

District Attorney's salary. I guess I figured that out when I saw all the monthly deposits he was making. By the way, Drew will be referring Cyril Green to the licensing board and the D.A.'s office to investigate. He'll be looking into the sources for the other payments, too."

"Wow," Millie said, shaking her head. "Sounds like we've given him a lot to clean up."

"So, what about us as we look ahead to the future?" Alex asked. "I mean, I hope we stay in touch and have a reunion sooner than in another ten years."

Rosemary spoke up. "No matter how many years it may take, I'll always feel close to you all after what we've been through and how much you've helped me."

"We became good friends during the four years we lived together at Woodley," Dottie commented. "We had some great times there."

Millie mimicked playing a violin. "Should we sing our school song to honor our alma mater?"

"Does anyone remember the words?" Alex asked. "Let me try. Here goes:

'High tower above us, thy columns so fair,

Gleaming white in their calm majesty;

Thus, long have they battled the wild storms of time

And will stand in the years yet to be.

Though we wander afar from thy sheltering walls,

Borne along on life's rough surging sea,

Yet our hearts, Alma Mater, unchanging and true

Will be loyal and faithful to thee.'

I think there's another verse, but I that's enough. Have you ever heard a song that's soppier than that? You could get a sugar overdose just singing it."

"If you even *could* sing it," Rosemary added. "I don't know what key it's in, but only a lowland gorilla can screech those high notes."

"They could transpose it a step down so people wouldn't turn blue when they get to, 'Though we wander afar,'" Dottie suggested.

"Well, I'm glad we were all there," Josie said. "It was a fun time and we got a good education. Tomorrow, we're going back to our own lives that are a lot different from when we were last together. If we don't see each other for a few more years, what do you suppose we'll be doing then?"

"I think I'll still be teaching grade school," Dottie opined. "I enjoy the children and it puts me on the same schedule with my own kids, so it's perfect for me."

"Me, too," Josie agreed. "I work a lot more hours than classroom time, but I get off a couple months in the summer, which is nice. What about you, Millie?"

"I'd like to stay in the news business, but maybe stop travelling so much. My dream job would be as a news anchor on TV. Maybe, too, to get married. What about you, Rosemary?"

"I need to get past selling the house and finding another place to live and getting resettled. I'd also like to stay in my job counselling kids, and, hopefully, marry down the road and maybe have a child of my own. Mitch never wanted children, so that's been a regret of mine. Okay, Alex, you're last. What's something you would want to do in the future?"

"Like all of you, I enjoy my job and want to continue to escort groups to places around the world for a long time yet. At some point, I'd like to try writing novels using my true-life adventures for my stories. I can see how the happenings of this week would make a great murder mystery; with all of you here during Mardi Gras, and the haunted Inn, and the tunnel, and Maria, and everything. As they say about bizarre things that happen in real life: 'You just can't make this stuff up.'"

THE END

ACKNOWEDGEMENTS

I'm grateful for all the help I've received in writing this book:

I want to thank my husband, Jim, for agreeing to spend several days in Mobile, Alabama, staying at the Malaga Inn, in order for me to research the area and learn about the local customs, particularly their extended Mardi Gras celebrations. The Civil-War era Malaga Inn is supposedly haunted, although we didn't see any evidence of spirits when we stayed there. (Full disclosure: I did not go down into the tunnel, but did look down the hole.)

I also want to thank Jim for encouraging my writing and giving me the space and privacy I need to complete my projects. He is my first reader whose comments about the characters and the story line have helped me to keep everything on track.

Thanks to my friends in the Authors Guild of Tennessee who continually support and take an interest in my writing.

I want to especially thank my friends John and Marilyn Neilans, who generously agreed to professionally edit and proofread my manuscript which has been greatly improved with their suggestions.

Lastly, I want to thank my friends from Hood College: Dottie Byerly, Kandy Higinbotham, Ruth Jones, and Milli Fazey, who are the inspirations for the central characters in my story. They have allowed me to use their actual, or thinly disguised, names for identification purposes. In turn, I have endeavored to portray their true personalities as well as their physical appearances from when we were in school.

The incidents I related during the time we lived in Terrace House (in Chapter 2) are true and accurate to the best of my recollection.

The dialogue and actions described relating to the murder mystery are purely from my imagination, based on my what I thought these friends would say and how they'd act given the fictional situation I have created. Even so, I'm sure I've fallen short in capturing their intellect and wit.

One special note: it was Dottie Byerly who gave me the idea to use her and the others from Terrace House in an Alex Trotter mystery.

It has been a joy for me to reflect back on my friendships with these women and to reference our good times together at Hood that enrich this story.

It is our hope that the five of us will be able to have an actual reunion sometime during the year following the publishing of this book.

Made in the USA
Columbia, SC
21 March 2021

34341724R00126